LOST

R.S. Guthrie

For my readers.
To authors, you are the lifeblood;
we admire no one more.

ACKNOWLEDGEMENTS

I want to thank my de facto editor, Elise Stokes. You are a fantastic author in your own right, and I owe you a deep debt of gratitude for working painstakingly through the final drafts of this book in the eleventh hour, never complaining yet always remaining impressively sharp. You were honest in dispensing astute, crucial editorial advice— more importantly, you did so because you cared so much about my book and my writing. I am profoundly grateful.

Thank you to Becky Illson-Skinner, Trish Gentry, and my lovely wife Amy for proofing my book. As a writer, it's amazing how many mistakes we leave in the wake of our creation. Each of you helped me to minimize mine.

Finally, to my readers. Without you, I would not write. You are the ears for which I compose my song. That you honor me by reading what I have written, giving me such wonderful feedback, and waiting patiently for my next book instills in me the greatest pride an artist can attain. These books are always, ultimately, for you.

PROLOGUE

"Whoever fights monsters should see to it that in the process he does not become a monster. And when you look long into an abyss, the abyss also looks into you."
~Friedrich Nietzsche

OVER TWO thousand children are reported missing every day, the largest percentage taken by family members. In other words, people they know: estranged fathers and mothers, grandparents, aunts, uncles, even siblings. In some of these cases we can sympathize, if not condone.

However, there are abductions every day that are not the act of a spurned ex or a frustrated grandparent. In these cases, the most innocent amongst us are taken by monsters; evildoers with no intention beyond causing harm to their victims. Too often, the harm comes in the form of torturous, unspeakable acts.

When we read about such heinous, willful disregard for young life—or for *any* life at all—we'd like to deny that the Universe could possibly contain such evil. Unfortunately, we all know that it does. What is more shocking to contemplate is where this evil exists—in other words, inside of *whom?* The church pastor? The manager at the supermarket? The nice teacher from the school down the street? How many times do we see people on the news, talking about yet another "average" neighbor being escorted from his or her home in handcuffs?

Amongst us at any given time, either feigning innocence or hiding undetected in the gray fog of the peripheral walks raw, consecrated evil. We break bread with these people. Invite them into our homes. Too often, entrust them with the care of our children.

The sane mind wants to know if it is possible for such evil to have evolved from within our own human ancestry. The answer is a complicated one. People are unique in this capacity; nowhere else in the animal kingdom do beasts wantonly torture and kill their own for no greater need than self-pleasure. Nowhere else do predators turn to evil for the sake of evil. Instances of death outside humankind are almost benign, so tied are they to nature's will to survive. Food. Protection. Advancement. These are the motivators behind killing for other species.

So how is it that some human beings have evolved into pure specimens of evil? It is impossible to answer such questions without first engaging the possibility of evil as a force—an entity completely outside human existence; an external force in and of itself; a force as real as those in physics, except that this force is exerted constantly upon the human mind, heart, and, eventually, its very soul.

And, like the laws of any physical force, there must be an opposite. For there to exist such inordinate forces of evil, there must also exist counterbalancing forces of good. One cannot exist without the other.

So if we accept that there are forces of good and evil in the Universe, there is another unavoidable maxim:

It is on the game field of good versus evil that humans play out their finite existence.

1

A friend loves at all times, and a brother is born for adversity.
King Solomon, *Proverbs 17:17*

MY BROTHER Jackson and I have not spoken much over the years. The reasons are complicated, but in the end, it is in large part because we are far too alike. Human beings have such incredible difficulty coming to terms with their own imperfections; it is no surprise that we tend to clash hardest with those most like us.

It's not that Jax and I don't love each other. I certainly love him, and I know he would be there for me if the walls were ever to come crashing down. Both of us believe family is always there for you. Forever. No matter what you need.

We are only a few years apart. I am the oldest. We'd been friends, off and on, for many years. Through most of our young adult lives, in fact. But things eventually changed. We didn't exactly grow apart. It was more like old wounds stopped scabbing over, instead remaining diseased and festering.

That has been the hardest truth for me to accept; two brothers who were once so close—the kind of friends that shared their innermost secrets—having become so irrevocably distant. Yet we had. Over the years we fabricated our own personal war—battles and skirmishes would appear and be waged at a moment's notice, and it seemed over the years that after such conflicts we receded into the frailty of friendship less and less often. Eventually we had to make some kind of peace; we were forced to face the fact that the emotional hurt we caused ourselves and those around us outweighed the value of the friendship.

Scotsmen tend to war within their own borders as well as without, and it is a wise general who recognizes the moment that a campaign becomes untenable.

So it had been a number of years since Jax and I had spoken regularly. We exchanged the obligatory greeting cards and holiday phone calls. I couldn't speak for my brother, but I learned a long time ago to release my heart's yearning for the days of yesteryear when my younger brother looked to me as his boon friend and confidant. In other words, I learned to accept the significance of the silence that had permeated our lives.

Therefore, when I saw the message on my desk from the P.A.A. telling me my brother in Idaho called and needed me to get back to him ASAP, I assumed bad news. He wouldn't call me at work otherwise.

I took the elevator down to the first floor and exited into the bright, sunny bustle of downtown Denver. It was a gorgeous day—the heart of the city beating beneath a vast, baby-blue sky dotted with fat, marshmallow clouds and a seasonal fall warmth that reminded me why I would always live in Colorado.

The nearest city bench looked as good as any spot to digest whatever my brother needed to tell me. I sat, but I did not call him right away. When faced with the prospect of speaking with Jax, I always made an attempt to calm myself first.

Later came the decompression.

"Chief Macaulay," the voice said.

"Hey, Jax."

"Bobby. How are you?"

He didn't seem upset. Unfortunately this realization did little to assuage the trepidation in my gut.

"Hanging in there," I said. "How's the family?"

"Trish's doing great," he said. "The little ones have grown. Celia is eight; Gracie just turned eleven."

"Like weeds, right?" I said, wondering where this uncharacteristic chewing of the rag was headed.

"I hesitated to call, but I've got a situation up here."

'Up here' was in Rocky Gap, Idaho—a small town in the panhandle of the state, not too far from Coeur d' Alene. My brother was the Chief of Police.

"Let's hear it," I said.

"Well, I can't divulge specifics. And I sure don't want you thinking we need some of that big city detecting up here. But I have to admit I could use your counsel."

"Go on."

"A local fella up and killed some of his family. Wife and one young daughter. I don't have to tell you how close that hits to home. Thing is, I know this guy. We all know him. He's not the family-murdering kind."

"It's been my experience there's no exact blueprint."

"Well, that's probably true in a lot of places," he said. "But I can tell you, here in Rocky Gap, you get to know folks."

"Understood," I said.

"I heard a little about what happened down there last year," he said.

"Heard what?"

"I have a couple of friends that moved down that way—

beat coppers. Word of the village has it you all ran into some pretty nasty characters in relation to a double-homicide. Sounds like maybe that one played a bit out of bounds."

"It was a strange one, all right," I said. "Not sure how that relates, though."

"You have any time coming?" he said. "I really could use you up here."

"I'm a little busy with casework," I lied.

"I've got this guy in my jail. He's going to stand trial for the whole truckload. Probably face a needle, and God knows, if he did what it looks like he did, I'd push the plunger myself. But he's got some pretty strange claims."

"Maybe he's thinking of an insanity defense," I said.

"Maybe. We've got the feds from Coeur d' Alene coming up here every other day, scratching at the back door wanting in. I'd like to get this thing taken care of locally—I know you get that."

"Look, Jax, I don't know what you've heard, but I doubt very much if anything that happened down here draws parallel to a guy going stir crazy in the sticks and taking out his entire family."

"Part of his family," he said.

"What?"

"I said *part* of his family. There's one member gone missing."

"Missing?"

"An eleven-year-old girl."

"Jesus."

"The father claims the Devil took her."

I let the words hang there in the stratosphere a moment. I really didn't want them to ever come down to earth.

"No kidding," he said. "I don't know what to do with

this one."

"I might be able to swing a week or two," I said.

"This guy, he's normally so sane it'd bore you to tears."

"We all have our breaking point. This little girl, how long's she been gone?"

"Three days," he said. "We think she may be in the Coeur d' Alene wilderness."

I felt like throwing up.

2

MEYER WEST, my cousin, the ex-priest, convinced me to drive the 1,222 miles from Denver to Rocky Gap. He was right. Flying didn't seem like a wise option. It was clear I needed to bring the Crucifix of Ardincaple—the family heirloom that had saved our lives in the forest around Grand Lake, Colorado. I still wasn't sure that I would be able to command the power of the weapon again, mainly because I had no fucking clue how I'd mastered it the first time. It was more like the weapon mastered *me*.

But we needed to bring it. And we weren't about to entrust its care to bag throwers at two different airports.

Meyer and I talked in depth about the night at Grand Lake. Calypso. Father Rule. The demon horde. Not easy things to reconcile. The mind is tempted when faced with the unbelievable to construct barriers of explainable alternatives. Meyer's calm acceptance of the preternatural made my own acceptance less cumbersome, if not easy. Meyer helped me come to grips with what had happened, though he himself admitted to having his own doubts as to what really occurred. Time has a way of eroding our confidence and even adding false memories to events. But still, his camaraderie was important to me. I had become very close with my cousin in that past year. Because of my splintered relationship with my only brother, I believe Meyer's companionship arrived at exactly the right time. Not only did I need a comrade, I also needed a friend.

Like Burke, my deceased partner, Meyer was an anachronism. Both of them were born out of time. Burke would have been much better suited to the era when men opened car doors without being scolded for it—a time when men were gentle and austere rather than triathlon competitors, weekend warriors, and Wall Street swindlers. And as for my cousin, how many children would tell you they want to be a priest when they grow up? All Meyer ever wanted was to serve the world in the name of God. The betrayal by his own mentor, Father Rule, had extinguished a light in him he believed could never flicker. Rule's evil had not driven Meyer West from the priesthood because it made him question his faith (although it would be foolhardy to believe it had not)—rather, my cousin felt he had failed; he felt responsible for Rule's successes. Meyer was shamed that he had not somehow seen through the ruse of the monster.

My cousin had always held things inside, divulging only what was necessary. After realizing how thoroughly the wool was pulled over his trust and faith, he became even more withdrawn and prone to turn from companionship rather than to seek it. I had to admit, I liked him all the more for it. He cared enough to sacrifice a part of himself to a cause and he felt responsible for the things in his world. In my estimation, these truths made him all the more approachable. More human. I placed an inordinate amount of trust in him right from the beginning. That's not something a Scotsman does easily. I learned that from my father, Paddy Macaulay, who only ever let a handful of men close enough to really know him.

In the Marines we called it *The Nine*.

"Fuck all but The Nine.

Six to carry the casket.

Two as road guard.

One to count cadence."

I already considered my cousin part of that select group.

"You're kind of quiet," I said to him, just south of Wilson, Wyoming.

"Mother Theresa taught her followers that God cannot be found in noise and restlessness."

"I guess that explains a lot."

"How so?"

"My own relationship with the Lord. Fractured, at best."

"I think you are closer to him than you realize."

"Maybe."

"The fact that you are willing to consider the possibility gives me hope," he said.

Faith was always a tough rubric for me. I grew up as a pragmatist and a bit of a Missourian. I like the tangible. Questions with answers.

The laws of the physical Universe.

The odds at the craps table.

Divorce rates.

This belief structure based on pragmatism made the Calypso case, what we all witnessed, and more importantly the surprising claims regarding my family history, that much more implausible to the logicians in my head.

The ability of erasure our grounded mind wields is impressive.

"Define distance," I said.

"God's distance does not necessarily relate to our own concepts."

"How so?"

"Everything we consider is based on our own paradigm—the lenses through which we view humanity, the Universe, even time."

"Okay."

"God's view is from a vantage point of omniscience."

"All seeing."

"All knowing," Meyer said, cracking the seal on a bottle of water from our ice chest. "God knows the permutations we've yet to consider."

"Faith is a human construct. We define it, not God," I said.

"Faith is a connection. It cannot exist in a vacuum. You can't connect to something that isn't there. Faith in another implies a relationship. It is a form of trust."

"But what of faith—or lack thereof—in the *existence* of a thing?"

Before he could answer, a little girl ran from the dense pine forest, across the slight barrow ditch, and directly in front of the truck. My reactions were gelatinous, having been lullabied into apathy by several hours of Wyoming nothingness. As my foot moved instinctively to the brake, I realized there was not enough time or distance.

The mind is a funny thing. Given enough time, the brain would love to ponder such notions as a young girl having no place in the middle of godforsaken Wyoming in the middle of a Wednesday night. But in a moment of mortal decision, the mind reacts. Our nature takes control. Sink or swim. Turn or run down an innocent.

I cranked the wheel and my truck lumbered left,

18

crossing lanes, rubber crying out against the pavement. We missed the girl, but as I went onto the gravel shoulder of the far side, the back end started sliding and caught up with the front.

I resisted the instinct to overcorrect, kept the gas pedal mostly depressed, and let the sixty mile an hour sideways power slide continue. It was our only chance, though I'm pretty sure Meyer did not understand.

As the back end began to fishtail to the left again, I eased a bit off the gas and corrected by turning the wheel right to counterbalance the inertia building in the horizontal slide. After taking out a handful of mile-marker posts, and (thankfully) meeting no new oncoming traffic, we skidded to a stop with the front tires still on the edge of the two-lane blacktop.

My heart was thudding like a bass drum in my chest and my fingers were cemented to the steering wheel. I turned to Meyer, who opened the door, leaned out, and vomited his dinner on the frigid night earth.

"You were saying?" I asked him as he closed the door and wiped his mouth.

"What…in the name…of all that is sacred…was *that?*" he managed.

"I have no idea," I said, turning around to an empty road. "Where the hell is she?"

"Where is *who?*"

I glanced sideways at my cousin, who had obviously not fully recovered from his emasculating performance.

"Funny. You just keep wiping the bile from your chin."

"Did you fall asleep?"

"Give me a break. No, I did *not* fall asleep."

"You almost killed us."

"I'm not in the business of running down children."

Father West sat there in stunned silence. I now looked him full in the eyes. I saw the incredulity therein.

"You didn't see the girl."

Meyer just kept staring.

"She ran from the tree line. Sunday dress. White shoes. Locks of hair flying behind her. She ran like a fucking *track star*. What the hell are you staring at?"

"There is nothing in the road."

"Not now," I said, suddenly feeling stupid and distraught. *Had I fallen asleep? Could I have dreamed it?*

"I think we should pull in when we reach Wilson," Meyer said. "Get a room. We've been on the road too long."

I nodded, putting my truck back into gear.

What was happening to me? I was sure I had not fallen asleep, but it seemed there was no girl waiting in the road, and I doubted she would have returned to the forest (what sense would *that* make?).

Then it grew inside me, a realization that I'd just seen the girl we were meant to save. How exactly had I known it was her? It wasn't possible, of course. Not really.

But that didn't stop me from knowing it.

3

MY FATHER was a hero. Paddy Macaulay worked for the Denver Fire Department for thirty-seven years. He rose to the level of Lieutenant, largely on the reputation he built as a smart, tactical firefighter who saved lives and was well-liked by his own peers.

Jax and I grew up in our old man's considerable shadow. There was not always time for the two young Macaulay boys. Paddy's dedication and first priority was always to his smoke-eater brethren. My brother and I understood. We knew our father loved us. It wasn't about that. He made the same facts clear to our mother when he married her; he may as well have been born into the fire department. He lived to serve his city and he couldn't change who he was or what he believed even if he had wanted to.

I always respected him for his honesty, in part because I'd always felt the same desire to serve (though it took me some time to finally understand the nature of that calling). I don't think Paddy knew anything about the family history—about the legends of the Clan MacAulay. If he did, he never shared it with me. When he got sick, the cancer took its time with him. He went into remission twice. I sat by his hospital bed on more occasions than I could remember. We had many chances to bring up the things that needed to be said between a father and son.

Yet he rarely spoke of our family history, and he didn't offer any new information before he died. I'll never know for sure what that means, but he may have been protecting me from my own destiny.

Either way, I missed him. I wanted to talk to him about all that had happened in my life since he died. We certainly could have had some deep discussions about the family genes.

Jax and my father were never very close, and they developed an even more damaged relationship near the end of Paddy's life. Not long after our mother's death—which was almost a decade before Paddy learned of his cancer—Jax began to feel differently about our father's professional estrangement from the family. More specifically, he started to resent the distance the job had put between Paddy and our mother.

I understood his disappointment. There were times I felt the same. Ma never stood up for herself. Rather, she chose to stand behind her husband. She never complained. And she raised us boys to be the same way. She told me once she loved Paddy with all her heart and that people don't change. She knew who Paddy was when she married him, so she accepted the good and the bad.

Jax began to think he was Ma's defender, I think, and so he grew more distant from Paddy as the years went on. They never really had a breakdown—only a weakening of the relationship's structure. When Paddy died, Jax was there with him, too, so I don't think he harbored any regret.

I understood Paddy more than my brother did because I knew I was like my father in many ways. My relationship with my own son, Cole, had been strained since he reached the teenage years. My wife, Isabel, died of cancer while she was supporting my career. I saw now that her dreams had come in second, usually relegated to the back burner. My job came first to me. Like my father. I think it was in my blood.

It therefore came as no surprise that I fell so hard for Special Agent Amanda Byrne of the FBI. In her I'd found someone who loved the job as much as I did. Two peas in a law enforcement pod. I didn't have to worry about her cursing my dedication to my career, nor did she have to worry the same about me.

~ ~ ~

Meyer and I had settled into our hotel room in Wilson, Wyoming. The wind moaned through the valley and whipped against the side of the building, sounding as if it might shake the walls until they gave in. I had much on my mind. The girl in the road and my certainty of who she was—or at least what she represented.

"Are you all right, Mac?"

"I've been thinking about Cole."

"It is not flesh and blood, but heart which makes us fathers and sons," Meyer said.

"Marcus Aurelius?"

"Friedrich von Schiller."

"It's a nice notion," I said. "But I doubt von Schiller understood the twenty-first century teenager."

"Good point."

"I worry about Cole. College should be a fun time. The boy has dealt with more tragedy than he should have."

"He's like you, Mac. He's strong."

"There's a difference between being strong and being *forced* to be strong."

"He'll be all right. Are you sure this isn't more about your relationship with your son than it is about his wellbeing?"

Typical Meyer. Cut to the quick.

"Probably," I said. "We used to be close. Now, after last year—losing his mother *and* Greer..."

"Methinks thou talks more of thyself than the boy," Meyer said.

"I need to walk," I told my cousin.

"I need to sleep," Meyer replied. "Go clear your head; it will do you some good. But please—do walk, don't drive."

I nodded and put on a light jacket. Outside the temperature was dropping fast. Thin, smoky clouds veiled the incandescence of the half moon, casting a dull glow on the land surrounding the hotel. I climbed out of the parking lot and toward the tree line, picking my way through the small rocks, twisted scrub, and up the steep grade.

The ground leveled some once I reached the stand of evergreens and I followed an old trail, away from the hotel. There was enough collateral light from the row of hotels along the main road by the interstate that I could see fairly well when my eyes adjusted. The small foot trail stayed parallel to the tree line and hotel row.

A couple of miles into the walk, I stopped to catch my breath. My lungs were attesting to the difference in altitude. I sucked in oxygen through my nose, willing my pulse to drop.

Then just as the pounding inside my ears subsided, I heard a large animal move in the forest to my right, snapping a large limb as it tried to pass. An elk, perhaps. I then heard another. And another. A herd? Unlikely this close to town, though wilderness seemed to encircle us there.

The noises grew more pronounced, less veiled. My stomach sank as I realized whatever was out there was coming for me. Wild creatures were more careful than this. The only animals that made such a racket when approaching were either unaware of the presence of others or they simply did not care. Such indifference normally implied a confidence in numbers, strength, or both. The sounds coming from inside the tree line seemed intentional. Confidently so.

Father Fic Rule stepped from the darkness directly ahead of me, along with half a dozen lesser demons on either side of him. Cruel, misshapen things. Dark as pitch; nearly invisible in the ethereal light.

Rule, who once masqueraded as a priest, believed he was indeed Satan on earth. He looked as evil and terrifying as the first time he appeared to me in my Denver home. His face and hands looked as if he'd survived some kind of terrible fire, most of his flesh having either melted away or melded with the underlying bone structure, giving him a skeletal appearance.

"You aren't really here," I said to him, hoping it was true.

"Believe what you must," the gravelly voice responded. "It matters not what you think. What matters is I am who I am."

"Have you been working on that opener since the last time we spoke? Because it needs work. More sincerity, maybe."

"The days of smart talk and complacency draw nigh to

a close, cop."

"Now you're sounding more like Calypso. Is he out there someplace with you, Rule?"

"They are *all* here with me. Your time is running out."

"You going to kill me right here, in the middle of Wyoming? That's not very biblical."

"I make the times and the places. I make all you see around you. This is not your God's world, or even your own. It is *mine*."

"Fine. Do your worst. Dream or no, I'm not afraid of you. You're a ghost. A specter of imagination. Your power can only go as far as it is given to you."

"You cannot choose my fate," he said. "But I shall command yours."

"Just words," I said. "Here are my words to you, beast: *go fuck yourself.*"

I turned to walk away, or wake up, whichever was next. Rule was instantaneously in front of me, as if materializing from the dew of night. He blocked my way, leering with those curled, pointed, blackish teeth.

"I could tear your soul from within. Right now. End it."

I pressed my nose against the gnarled flesh where his nose should have been. It felt tender and cold, like hamburger just pulled from the cooler.

"Then do it," I said. "I told you. I am not afraid of you."

Rule raised both his arms and the throng of demons descended all around me as a crowd suddenly swells and traps one of its own. The creatures were indeed hideous, and my courage began to wane.

"With one passing thought I could release their rage; give them what they so desire," he said, pallid eyes locked with my own. "They wouldn't leave so much as a splinter of bone."

"End it, then," I said.

He lingered there, his hatred of me palpable.

And then, without a breath of sound, the horde retreated into shadow, leaving only Father Rule and me.

"Not here," he whispered into my ear, wheezing through those mangled holes in the middle of his face. "Not until you've mourned the children."

With that, he vanished, leaving me to shiver against the cold of night.

R.S. GUTHRIE

(

4

THE VOICE had been directing Spence Grant's actions for several months. It was difficult now, remembering when it had first begun to goad him along.

His family didn't know, though he always suspected Gloria—his wife and sweetheart since the eighth grade—might have wondered a bit about his odd behavior in the days leading up to the murders.

Spence ignored the voice for more than a week. Maybe more than two. At first he honestly believed he was hearing something else. He thought he'd accidentally eavesdropped on one side of a nearby conversation, not unlike a baby monitor that picked up a stray signal. After all, it began as a whisper in the night, slightly more profound than the wind rustling a small scattering of leaves. He'd not understood exactly what was being said until a few nights later.

You know things are not as they seem.

And still he resisted. Only crazy people heard someone speaking who wasn't there. And anyone who answered— or God forbid acted upon such ephemeral suggestion— was certifiable.

But the voice made sense; that was the rub. A *lot* of sense.

Things are not as they seem.

The world has gone to Hell and no one is going to do anything

29

about it.

YOU *need to do something about it, Spence.*

When the voice inside called him by name, *that* got his attention. Spence started thinking about what the voice was telling him. He thought about it a lot. And he also started smiling at the oddest moments.

The voice spoke to him throughout the day, off and on, but mostly it serenaded him at night, in the dark, when the stresses of the day had dissipated like smoke in a stiff wind. It waited until his palate was cleansed—his canvas white and willing.

Eventually he came to covet the voice. Depend upon it. Cleave to its wonderful logic. After a time it became clear the voice was one of purpose, one of mettle. It became clear it would dictate his way forward, and Spence wanted that. He *needed* direction.

The first call to action played into Spence's view of the world about him. It was necessary, the voice told him, to slake the thirst of one's own needs.

Spence Grant hated someone. A very putrid someone. A woman named Della Gerard. He was not alone in his hatred, he knew. Gerard was a nasty little woman, a crossing guard for the girls' school in the morning who then directed the pickup of the children in the midafternoons.

Half the township had it in for Della Gerard.

The woman was a fine example of what occurred when a hen-pecked youth grew up and grabbed hold of even a *sliver* of power—a sconce of dominion over others; one that she could wrap her spindly little fingers around and wield like a scythe to all who opposed her.

Spence had said on more than one occasion that she ran the pickup zone like a prison soup kitchen—pointing her baton this way and that, chewing on the parents, most who had just rushed in from one stress-filled job or another and didn't much appreciate the mousy dictator and her oppressive little fiefdom.

So one night a few weeks before the murders, the voice told Spence a funny anecdote:

Did you hear about the noxious bitch with a chip on her shoulder that got herself run over by a well-meaning parent? Her chip isn't nearly as big anymore.

Spence found he liked that story. Liked it a lot, in fact. Liked it so much when his brain went to making it more of a *plan* than a funny piece of indulgent fiction, he found he didn't have much of a problem with the idea at all.

The next midafternoon, when Della Gerard was holding him back with a flat palm and grousing at a parent who'd been parked a few seconds too long in the yellow zone, Spence simply eased off the brake pedal, turned the wheel ever so slightly, and let the right front wheel of his rusted Subaru Forrester run up and over the foot and ankle of his least favorite crossing guard, snapping her tibia and fibula like brittle summer branches in a rainless wood.

At the hospital, Spence apologized emphatically and even managed to produce a few tears when being interviewed by the Chief of Police. The incident was ruled an unfortunate accident, and though Spence's insurance premiums went through the roof, Della Gerard retired from her policing duties and never walked correctly or without pain again.

~ ~ ~

Killing didn't come as easy to Spence. Most murderers needed to warm up to the idea. Even serial killers began slowly, sometimes graduating from assault to rape to murder. The voice convinced Spence Grant that he could prey on some of God's lesser creatures to ease his trepidation.

The voice questioned him relentlessly:

What about medical science? Labs do heinous things to rats and mice and even guinea pigs, Spence. All under the guise of saving the world from the disease and pestilence brought about by themselves. Why not you? If you aren't committed to changing the way things are, then...

But Spence *was* ready to learn. Or at least he then believed what had to be done *had to be done*. He just needed some practice. So he bought a dozen mice, four rats, and two gerbils at a pet store in Coeur d'Alene.

Spence hated rodents. He would never be talked into hurting a dog, or even a cat.

The voice was specific about the practice runs.

Look each of them in the EYE, Spence. Taking a life is a personal thing. Look each of them in the eye, and you won't be afraid. Put YOUR fear into THEM, Spence. Send them on their way.

Spence looked each mouse in the eyes. He knew it would be different with a *person*. The mice had no reasonable sentience. They were terrified, which helped, but they sensed only basic, overarching danger. They could not possibly know what the scalpel held in store for them.

~ ~ ~

Three days before the murders, Spence hadn't heard from the voice in a week, and he was getting edgy. It was clear the voice meant him to graduate to a human being, and the idea of taking the life of one of his own kind had actually become a bit of a fixation. After all, mice were not culpable in the destruction of the world.

Men were.

And women.

His own people.

It was finally time to make a difference. The voice didn't have far to go in convincing him of that.

Yet Spence still didn't know who the first victim would be. This had him pacing back and forth in the downstairs study when his wife thought he was working through the family finances. Who would it be?

Then, at three thirty-three in the morning, exactly seventy-two hours before the murders, the voice returned to him to give him the plan.

You must kill THEM, it said to him.

Who? Spence asked the voice.

You know who.

He *did* know.

But I want to make a difference, Spence said. He didn't want to be a monster; he wanted to rid the world of the bad people.

Not his own *family.*

You cannot rid the world of monsters, Spence. The world will always have them. But you can send good people away from here— far, far away. To a better, monster-less place!

It made sense. The world was no better than a ring of Hell. How many times had he questioned the decision of bringing two young girls into the cesspool of what now passed as "humanity"? He'd never considered such an act of finality in his deliberations, of course. But what a few months before would have been impossible to even imagine, now appeared preordained and positively resplendent.

~ ~ ~

As Spence tucked his two angels away beneath the patchwork covers that night he could hardly contain his excitement for them. His hands were shaking he was so impatient to send them on their journey. What greater thing could a father do than remove his children from a life sentence in Hell?

And his wife. It made him warm inside to think of her going first. She would be waiting for the little ones, and then, finally, for him—when the four of them could transport themselves a billion light years away from all the mess the world had become; they would leave this toilet of a civilization and disappear into cosmic bliss in the wink of an eye.

The act of sharpening the knife was more than symbolic. Great patience was the key. He moved the edge along the rough whetstone, careful not to nick the blade. Over and over he lovingly pulled the blade, honing, perfecting.

He'd purchased the knife a few days earlier, though he'd been looking for the perfect weapon for a long time—nosing in and out of cutlery shops, attending gun shows, frequenting flea markets.

So many wonderful knives; so many choices.

The voice inside assured him he would know the right talisman when he found it. The one. The blade that

34

would draw his family closer to God; closer to Paradise.

And he *did* know it. He found it in a smallish, private shop on a trip across the border to Missoula on business. An old Nez Perce woman ran the store, which exhibited twenty to thirty blades attached to meticulously carved handles made from alabaster, elk horn, and obsidian.

Spence knew the moment he saw the magnificent black handle, the curved deboning blade glinting even in the dull light of the little shack. When he saw it he forgot why he ever drove to Missoula in the first place. Did he not come for this?

Of course you did, the voice assured him.

"How much," he asked the wrinkled old woman.

"Two hundred," she said. "Handmade. Very strong."

No price seemed too high for the tool he needed. He paid the woman.

The voice was speaking to him again, saying he'd better make sure there were no loose ends. It was, after all, a small shop. And the voice seemed to have a problem with the broken down Indian woman.

She is shaman, Spence. A child of the coyote. Seer. Look into her eyes. She already knows. One phone call to the locals and your plan is over—your children struggle through decades of living Hell.

Spence *did* look into the old, wrinkled face. Into those cloudy, ancient orbs, devoid of compassion. The voice was right. It was clear she knew.

A shaman.

Just his luck. But then again, he thought, where else to find a knife to do God's work? Not Wal-Mart.

Spence had been palming the knife, admiring it, when the voice told him about the Indian medicine woman. He kept his eyes locked on hers as he reached across the counter, grabbed a fistful of her long, gray-streaked hair, and pulled her toward him. She drew a deep breath, as if to cry out, and Spence deftly plunged the knife into her esophagus, silencing any scream that may have been building.

He remembered his practice. He kept his own eyes locked on the Indian woman's. He watched as the fight drained from her gaze; he stared as the life went out of her.

There were no cameras. No security personnel. It was a small shop, run by poor, proud people. Spence lowered the old woman, inanimate, down into the pool of her own chocolate-colored blood. The vessel was no longer aware, but Spence smiled knowingly, happy he could send another proud, decent soul onward, away from a world filled with horror and shame.

5

AMANDA BYRNE occupied my thoughts. Three-quarters of a continent away and still I could not forget her. Not that I wanted to. I don't know about such things being preordained, but the moment I saw her I knew I'd never be able to resist. The smoothness of her skin, the flame red hair, those bottomless green eyes. I missed her.

It sounds shallow to mention her in terms of her external beauty. I realize it's uncouth to do so, but I have never been able to deny that the most beautiful creatures are the most desirable. Yes, there is more. Far more. Beauty is, at best, skin deep. But God, or evolution, or whatever mechanism you have conceded dominion over our existence, burned into us a need to mate with the strongest, or most physically dominant, of our species. We are all attracted to innate beauty.

Such attraction should not be overpowering—so inexplicably intoxicating— but often we are not in control of the innate, feral needs that rise up against our better judgment. We put up the good fight; we assure ourselves and others that we are in control. But it has been my experience that control of our lives is, at best, an illusion, and at worst, an unattainable obsession.

I called Amanda as soon as I decided to travel to Idaho to help my brother. I told myself it was a professional call. Not a chance. I needed to hear her voice. I wanted to see her again. Her interest in me had seemed to lessen with the distance between us, or at least that is how I read it. There was a flatness in her voice when we talked. And it seemed the frequency of our calls was also diminishing.

"Amanda, it's Bobby."

"Bobby. How have you been?"

That flatness again. I wished it was my imagination, but I knew better. I was a detective. I counted on my ability to hear such things.

"Casework has been slow," I said. "You?"

"The Bureau has me buried in bullshit paperwork. Life of a fed."

"I've missed you," I said. Amateur hour. The knee-jerk reaction of Insecure Lover.

"Me, too."

Classic non-response.

"Listen, my brother called from Idaho. He needs my help on a case up there."

"What kind of case?"

"A little girl has been abducted."

"Oh my God."

"He feels a fresh set of eyes might help."

"Are you going?"

"I don't think I have a choice."

"There's always a choice."

"It's more than that. There are some uncomfortable similarities with the Calypso case."

"No shit?" she said. I had her attention now.

"The girl's mother and sister were murdered. By the father."

"Doesn't sound much like the Calypso case."

"The father says the Devil took her."

"Hmm."

"You don't sound impressed," I said.

"I see the parallel now."

"Yeah, I know. It's thin. But I have some time coming and things are slow here."

"Look, Bobby...I have been meaning to talk to you. I feel like I owe you an explanation."

"You don't owe me anything."

"I've been intentionally distant."

"I noticed."

"I'm sorry. It's not you."

The 'it's not you, it's me' line. I thought we'd moved deeper than second date repertoire.

"I've had so much on my mind," Amanda said.

"I get it. We shared some time together. Great while it lasted. Maybe we thought it was going to be more. Or maybe I did."

"I'm pregnant."

The merry-go-round stopped. It didn't slow down; the ride ended so hard my head nearly separated from its axis.

"Shit," was all I could think to say. "Sorry."

It wasn't my finest moment.

"It's okay," she said. "My reaction was about the same. To be honest, Bobby, I have been thinking for a long time about what I should do."

"What *we* should do, I'd like to think."

"Of course. I'm sorry."

I was in New York four months earlier, at her request. She took a week off work and we stayed downtown in a four-star hotel, her showing me the city, us making love and ordering room service. It wasn't long after my return that she started clamming up.

"I wanted to tell you, Bobby. Something inside me needed distance; needed to digest this notion before breaking the news to you."

"Meet me in Idaho," I blurted out.

"What?"

"Fly there. Help me sort out what's going on with my brother. It will give us some time together."

"You want me there?"

"Of course I want you there," I said. "Both of you."

"Jesus, Bobby. I want to cry. I don't have to tell you how messed up that is for me. It confuses me."

"What did you think, Amanda? I was going to stop calling you?"

"Maybe. Something like that. I'm a strong woman. I would have dealt with it."

"But you don't *have* to deal with it."

"Okay."

"I'm in love with you, lady."

There was a long pause on the line.

"Fuck you, Bobby Mac. Fuck you for making me feel like a schoolgirl after her first kiss."

"I have a way with women."

More silence. Then:

"I love you, too."

~ ~ ~

In the quiet of the house all I could think about was the new life growing inside Amanda and, frankly, what a baby meant to us, our world, and to me as a past-forty cop who was closer to breaking down than to the glory days of old.

I *did* love Amanda. It was the first time I'd told her that, however. Her reaction was certainly positive enough—more so than I'd hoped. She loved me, too.

That fact alone instilled a confidence in me that had been missing for some time. Just over a year ago I'd said the same words to another woman—Greer Foster: college professor, dog lover, and part-time Bobby Mac fan. I say *part time* because I think it could be argued that I was more filler in her life than something (or someone) she ever really considered a permanent fixture.

In other words, I had fallen hard for her, too, but was unsure if she felt the same toward me. I would never find out; I'd never know if there was room for me in the world she was hammering out for herself. Greer's death was harder even than losing my wife, Isabel. I thought Greer was the one; the woman to fill that void in my life, give me more children, and share the rest of my life with me. When she died, as with Isabel, a part of Bobby Mac died with her.

~ ~ ~

The relationship with my brother is a conundrum I've struggled to reconcile since I was old enough to wonder about such things. How can two boys be so similar and share such joy while at the same time being predestined to destroy each other?

Jax and I were like matter and antimatter.

Meyer and I drove down Main Street toward the old brick two-story in Rocky Gap that housed the town police department.

"You and your brother were close once," Meyer said.

"We were."

"You've never said what drove you apart."

"Probably because there is no one thing," I said.

I wish it *had* been one thing. A disagreement. A wrong that needed righting. *Things* can be fixed. It's not so easy to restructure what is coded into our DNA.

"I always wanted a brother," Meyer said. "You are lucky to have Jax."

"It doesn't always feel that way. He and I are too much alike. We aren't good for each other."

"Isn't it more complicated than that?"

"Not really."

I pulled the truck into a visitor spot and killed the engine. It occurred to me this was the first time I'd visited my brother since he became Chief. When he was a patrol officer, I flew up for the birth of Gracie. Even then it was clear to me he'd be running the department one day. My brother was a good cop. We had that in common, too.

Jax was at the front desk, waiting on our arrival, drinking from a large mug of steaming coffee. Our father loved his java, too. The bitter stuff never did much for me.

"Bobby," Jax said as we walked through the double glass doors. He extended a meaty paw. My brother was several inches taller than I was and outweighed me by twenty or thirty pounds. I accepted his iron grip.

Macaulays did not hug.

"Meet Meyer," I said.

"Ah, the priest," Jax said, offering a second handshake.

"Retired," Meyer said.

"Once of the cloth always of the cloth," Jax said to him. "Cops don't retire, they die. Same thing in your line of work."

Apparently bluntness ran in the family, too.

"You are a cousin, too?"

"So they say," Meyer said.

Jax motioned down the hallway.

"Let's sit in my office."

~ ~ ~

"We've got search parties working around the clock," he said, pointing to a map of the Coeur d'Alene wilderness. "Teams of forty. Sweeping the area. Divers working the rivers and lakes."

"What makes you think she's been abducted?" I said. "Could your perp have killed her, too? Buried her to assuage his guilt?"

"Not possible," Jax said. "Melissa Grant called us."

"What do you mean 'she called you'?"

"Two nights after we put the father in the jail, my office received a call from a blocked number. We believe it was her."

"You *believe*."

"We analyzed the recording. According to the software, it was not an exact voice match. But I'm telling you it was her. The caller knew things only Melissa Grant could have known."

"For example?"

"A detailed account of what her father did to her mother and sister. Specifics we've not released anywhere."

"Could be an accomplice."

"Not in a murder suicide deal."

"Why do you call it that?"

"It's all in my interview with Spence Grant, the father."

"And you think she's been taken to the Coeur d'Alene wilderness?" Meyer said.

"The abductor told us where he was taking her."

"You spoke to him?" I said.

"He got on the call after the girl. Said that we'd never find them, not in an eternity of searching."

"He said that? Used 'eternity' in that context?" I asked him.

"Yeah. Exactly like that. Why?"

"It has a familiar ring."

"The bastard even gave us his name."

The warmth drained from my body. A name? Eternity? All I could think was *Calypso*. But it couldn't be him. Not in this world.

"What was the name?"

"Annir," Jax said.

A wave of relief washed over me.

"Does that name mean anything to you?" I said.

"Not a thing."

"I know it," Meyer said. "It's from a poem in the Book of Ossian entitled *Cath-Loda*".

"You're kidding," I said.

"What book?" Jax said.

'The Book of Ossian. A collection of poetic tales handed down through the Scottish ages. Annir was an evil presence. To quote:

"A fire that consumed of old. He poured death from his eyes along the striving fields. His joy was in the fall of men. Blood to him was a summer stream, that brings joy to the withered vales, from its own mossy rock."

"Meyer has a bit of a photographic memory," I said.

"I gather," Jax said, unimpressed.

"He's studied many of the ancient Scottish texts," I

44

said. "It can be useful."

Meyer interjected, "Most of the lore was passed down by the spoken word. The poetry of Ossian is one of the only known written accounts."

"Whatever the man's name is," Jax said, "we're doing everything we can."

"Good," I said, anxious to change the subject. "When can I talk to Spence Grant?"

"You're not talking to Grant," Jax said. "Are you out of your mind?"

"You called *me* in."

"You've been here less than an hour."

"Like I said, you called me in."

"And don't make me sorry I did. This is my domain. Not the world according to Bobby Mac."

"Message received," I said. It was another of those times when it paid to back down. And it *was* his domain. His town, his department, his case.

"Look, I get you asking, I do. I'm just not convinced you interviewing the suspect is a good idea. We don't want to contaminate the case. Besides, I'd have to clear it with the County Attorney."

"Do me a favor then…just *ask*."

"Fair enough," Jax said. "Until then, I have the initial interview on DVD."

~ ~ ~

The interview was beyond chilling. Spence Grant told the story of how he butchered his wife and youngest daughter with the banality of a man reciting back the grocery list to make sure he didn't miss anything. I've talked to many murder suspects, and you learn quickly that nothing ought to be surprising. You give up trying to connect with the mind of someone capable of such brutality and unchecked evil. But Spence Grant was unlike any other I'd ever encountered. How could anyone be so matter-of-fact about the terrible acts he'd committed against those he ostensibly loved more than any other?

According to Grant, he used chloroform first on his sleeping family. Said he didn't want them to wake up again. But the chloroform was not what killed them. The voice told Grant that each death had to be personal—that he was charged with this sacred duty and that the method was as important as the act itself.

The wife went first. Grant used a curved deboning knife to cut her throat. He vividly recounted what it felt like, sitting there on the bed as her lifeblood streamed from her body and pooled around his legs and buttocks. He said the warmth filled him with such love for her.

Next Grant murdered his youngest daughter, Millie. He said he held her in his lap and used the same knife he'd used to kill his wife. Said he sliced his little girl from her stomach to her chin—describing the act as would an adorning father telling the story of opening a present Christmas morning.

The most intriguing part of the interview came when Jax asked him why he spared his oldest daughter, Melissa.

"I had not planned to," he said. "But I was informed there is still work for her before she joins the others."

Grant said his original intent had been to murder all of them and then take his own life. He told my brother the voice stopped him after the first two murders; told him to spare his eldest for a bigger plan.

6

THE COEUR D'Alene National Forest is one of three parcels of land that make up the Idaho Panhandle National Forest. It is extremely rugged country, populated by evergreen hills, craggy mountains, grizzly bears, and over half the state's surface water in lakes, rivers, streams, and tributaries. Truly one of the last places on earth you want to have to search for a person.

Or a body.

"Priest River?" I said to Jax in his office.

Meyer was cleaning up in the Men's room.

"What?"

I pointed to a spot on the map in his office. "There's a *Priest River?*"

"Just north of us."

"And Saint Joe National Forest?"

"Yep."

"Saints, priests...what is it with the land up here?"

"A lot of the French trappers and miners who settled this country were of Catholic descent. You should know that. It's your heritage as much as it is mine."

"Religion isn't heritage," I said. "It's a personal choice."

"Spoken like a true heathen."

"Don't give me that shit. I believe in God. That's enough for me."

"What if he doesn't believe in you?"

47

I thought about that one for a moment.

"I've never been that sure he does."

Jax pointed to my left leg.

"How's that working for you? The new leg that is."

The new leg. It was the most he'd said in ten years about my prosthetic, as if merely discussing it might bring the same misfortune down on him, too.

"It's given my profession back to me," I said.

"The department didn't give you any grief?"

"You know, typical bureaucratic nonsense…but ultimately, I proved to them I could handle the job physically."

"No more track star, though."

"Thanks for the reminder."

"No, just saying. Sorry."

"It's okay. Truth is I just received a new sprinter prosthetic last month. I've been training for a triathlon. Running the 400-meter again, actually."

"Bullshit."

"Before I left Denver, had my time down to sub sixty seconds."

"Damn, Bobby. That's great."

The newest leg had really completed my rehabilitation. Coming back to the force—making Detective, returning to full action—that had been a *huge* accomplishment. But there was a time when my running defined me. Basketball had always been something I was known for, but my days in track were the ones that stuck with me. My true love.

I ran the 400-meter and the anchor leg of the 1600-meter relay in college. Set a conference record of 47.2 seconds in the individual race that still stands today. In the years following college I nurtured the running into a distance and mountain trail regimen that had me hopeful to compete in the Iron Man triathlon in Hawaii one day before my fortieth birthday. Losing my left leg in the line of duty put an end to those dreams.

Until the Flex-Foot Cheetah. The Cheetah was designed by Össur, intended for use by both professional and recreational amputee sprinter athletes. South African Oscar Pitorius—"Blade Runner"; the fastest man on no legs—set the world Paralympic records in the 100, 200, and 400-meter running on a pair of Cheetahs.

"I'm really happy for you, Bobby. I hope you know that."

"It's made me feel whole again," I told him. "When I lost the leg—those first few months—I thought it was over. I thought *I* was over."

"I guess rumors of your demise were exaggerated?"

"Hell yes," I said.

~ ~ ~

Amanda arrived that evening and I met her at the small, two-runway airport. She looked amazing, walking that austere walk of hers, gliding across the blacktop, closing the distance between us with poise and effortlessness. When she was closer I could see her baby bump. She noticed me staring and her mouth curled in a sardonic smile.

"Don't say a word," she said. "I'll watch what I eat later on."

"You look great."

"Says you."

I kissed her softly.

"May I?" I said, looking down at her stomach.

She nodded, and I placed my palm over our child.

"Don't think this makes an honest woman of me," she said.

"I know better," I said, and kissed her again.

We drove to my hotel room and I made her dinner in the little kitchenette: sautéed pearl onions, baby potatoes, seared trout, and a pan of apple crisp. I retrieved an armload of split logs from the deck and we shared a sparkling apple cider basking in the warmth of a nice blaze in the wood-burning fireplace.

In the bedroom I slowly undressed her, running my palms against her alabaster skin, smooth as the surface of a polished stone. I pulled her nakedness against me and we molded together as one shape as we lowered to the pillow-top bed.

I kissed her red lips and she wrapped her arms around my back, drawing her nails softly across the span of my shoulders. Her breathing skipped and she sighed softly as I kissed the side of her neck, tugging on an ear lobe with my teeth.

The lovemaking fulfilled me, made me whole again. It was gentler this time, both of us wary of the new life growing within her.

Afterward, Amanda lying in my arms, we talked.

"You seemed tense when you called me last time," she said.

"I thought you were dumping me."

"I considered it," she said, smiling.

"You'd have been better off. I'm a lug."

"That's what I love about you, Mac. That, and the fact you are such a fucking pushover."

"Your New York accent has returned nicely."

"I look forward to you softening it."

"There are some things that even I cannot do," I said.

"Are you sure you're okay with all this?"

"I told you how I feel. I couldn't be happier."

"Thank you."

"For what?"

"For not knowing why I'm thanking you."

I kissed her again and wondered if we *should* be worried about the prospect of bringing another baby into a world where fathers listened to voices in their heads and were capable of cutting their little girls into pieces.

R.S. GUTHRIE

7

JAX TALKED to the County Attorney and he agreed to allow me an interview with Spence Grant. I was nervous about confronting the man who had murdered his own wife and daughter. I did not understand such heinous disregard for the things that are important in this life. We only get one pass through—when we are lucky enough to be given a wife who loves us, and a pair of beautiful daughters who adore us, it befalls us not to screw it up.

Still, I would be lying if I said Spence Grant did not intrigue me. First, even a homicide detective is capable of feeling awe toward a specimen like that. Second—and this one is hard for me to admit—the man was engaging, confident, and even strangely witty. It wasn't that I liked or admired him; those feelings would have been impossible. But I found that I also did not hate him. I really wanted to detest the man—his crimes went beyond unthinkable or unconscionable. Yet he elicited in me a false sense of camaraderie. And it angered me. Consequently I think I was too hard on him. The deputy who pulled me off Grant and then arrested me certainly agreed.

"Who are you?" he said when I entered the interview room.

He wasn't rude. His tone was that of a child asking the same question: pure, innocent curiosity.

"Detective Robert Macaulay."

"Jax's brother from Denver," he said. "I love that city. Gloria and I used to ski Winter Park every other year, before the girls were born. We'd stay at the Brown Palace on our first and last night in the city. Magnificent landmark hotel."

"Gloria. That was your wife."

"She's still my wife."

"That's a funny way to look at it," I said. "I think you put an end to the nuptials, Mr. Grant. With punctuation."

"Call me Spence. That's only because you are short-sighted, Mac."

"Detective, if you don't mind."

"No, of course not. No offense intended."

"Tell me a little more about you murdering your family."

"See, now you're trying to get a rise out of me."

"You seem surprised."

"I just don't understand why. I've already confessed."

"There's the matter of your missing daughter."

"Melissa's fine."

"Then you know where she is?"

"So do you. Not to be obtuse, Mac…er, Detective."

"On second thought, call me Mac."

"She's in the Coeur d'Alene wilderness, Mac."

"Did the man who took her tell you that?"

"Annir," Grant said. "He's no man. Not any longer."

"You told my brother—Chief Macaulay—that he was the Devil."

"Originally I thought he was. Not a nice soul."

"Yet you seem oddly at ease with her abduction."

"Again, not to be picky, but she wasn't abducted. Not really.

"Because you're okay with it?"

"Because I agreed to it, yes."

"Seems to me you might have been under some duress."

"Duress?"

"Annir sounds like someone accustomed to having his requests granted."

"That he is."

"Maybe you've had second thoughts since then."

"I'm fine with my decision. As parents, we are tasked with making the hard choices. Particularly ones a father makes for his little girls. When you have a daughter, you'll understand."

"How do you know I don't have a daughter?"

"Your brother told me you have one son."

"Yes, it's true."

"*Was* true, you mean."

"What does that mean?" I said.

"You have a daughter now. Growing inside your girlfriend."

"How the fuck…"

"I'm sorry, Mac. The voice told me."

He couldn't possibly know anything about the pregnancy. I hadn't even told Jax. And Amanda didn't know anyone here.

"How did you…?"

"I wish I could tell you how it works. Sorry to be so cryptic, but the voice, it doesn't have a name. I used to think it was just my conscience, but clearly that's not the case. I've never been clairvoyant."

"So the voice told you about my baby?"

"Your *daughter*," he said. "She's just the size of a peanut right now."

There wasn't so much as a flicker of surprise in Spence Grant's eyes when I came across the table and took him to the floor.

It was fortunate for me—and for Grant—that the interview was being monitored. Though I had no way of knowing, Jax had stepped out of the observation room and asked one of his deputies to take the witness role in his absence. Thank God the man was quick to react. I only had a few moments with the murderer beneath my fists, but it was enough time to do a lot of damage.

"DETECTIVE," Deputy Bill Severs shouted as he burst into the room and yanked me off the defenseless prisoner, who was then bleeding heavily from his lip, right ear, and broken nose.

Severs put me face down on the floor, cuffed me, and read me my rights.

Spence Grant never made a sound.

~ ~ ~

"What the HELL were you thinking," Jax asked me in his office, me still in plastic tie cuffs.

"Can you take me out of these?" I said.

"No, Bobby, I can't. The County Attorney is on his way over here. Bad news *flies* in this town. How the fuck do I even remotely explain this? Grant's attorney is going to be shooting at fish in a barrel on this one. He may even get his client released, do you realize that?"

"That's a crock. The man's a multiple murderer with victim number three still out there somewhere."

"This isn't the big city. Charges of brutality are taken seriously here in Smalltown, U.S.A."

"I get it. Do you think I spend my time in Denver kicking the shit out of my prisoners?"

"I honestly don't know. You had less than an hour with mine and couldn't keep your hands off him."

The County Attorney, Saul Xavier, came thundering into the precinct.

"Is this him?" he bellowed. "Is this the dipshit who just assaulted a prisoner in my custody?"

"He's in *my* custody, Saul. Sit down," Jax said, a lot calmer than he'd been just a moment ago. He walked around to me, motioned to give him access to my backside, and clipped the cuffs. I rubbed my sore wrists as Xavier went mad again.

"What the fuck do you think you are doing, Chief? Cuff that prisoner before I arrest you, too."

"You don't arrest people either. And if you don't pipe down, I'm going to have my deputies come in here and remove you forcibly. You won't like that at all, I promise."

Jax looked at me.

"Now why don't you start from the beginning, for Mr. Xavier's benefit?"

I shared the entire interview, which had also been taped. Afterward, Xavier wanted to view the twenty-two and a half minutes for himself.

"There's no way he could have known about the pregnancy," the attorney asked me later, after making a few calls.

"None," I said.

"I didn't even know," said Jax.

"Then how…" Xavier began. "Never mind. After we

watched the tape, I called Springer Lewis, Grant's attorney. He wasn't even aware of the incident, which is pretty shocking because Grant was taken to the emergency room for stitches and a resetting of his nose. Afterward he was given a phone call."

"Who did he call?" Jax said.

"Ewing's Auto Repair. To see when his wife's car would be ready. It was dropped off a few days before the murder. Merle Ewing said Grant just wanted to make sure the bill was paid on time and that no additional storage charges accrued."

"Jesus. He has no concept of what's happening all around him," Jax said.

"He knows," I said. "He's just pleased as frog shit that it's all going according to plan."

"Well, he's not pressing charges," Xavier said. "Springer is mad as hell because he can't talk his client into it. Grant's exact words were *I'd have beaten the tar out of me, too.* End quote."

8

I'VE FELT the Scotsman in my veins since bagpipes first beckoned to the ear of my soul. Paddy used to put me on his knee and we would listen to records on the old turntable, those once-outlawed pipes haunting me with songs of the old country.

I've never been able to fully explain it. I was born and spent my whole life in the United States—as American as they come—but there has always been a palpability to the feeling of Scottish heritage in my soul. I had yet to visit my homeland, but in the year after losing my partner and my girlfriend, I considered it more than any other time in my life. I wanted to see Scotland one day. I needed to climb to the top of the rolling mountains, as did William Wallace, whom my ancestors hid from British soldiers and fought next to as Scotland won her freedom.

The bulk of Father Terence Macaulay's journal—my *grandfather's* journal—had been stored away inside my head. I read much of it directly after Calypso was killed and my son healed. Father Macaulay was a complicated man. I never considered myself very complex, but I suppose he didn't either—or any complicated man, for that matter.

There was a particular passage that moved me; one that reached so far into my soul I knew I would never forget the words:

We don't choose our heritage, nor does it choose us. It simply IS. What we can do is respect it; we can carry on the traditions of our ancestors. We owe them as much. The Clan MacAulay is one of vital importance, and this dedication to duty—indeed the very genetic need to protect this world—has been passed to us as the torch is passed to the next sentry, ready to give his life for the rest of the land.

This genetic need to protect and to serve my fellow mankind has been with me since I can remember. It's not something taught but rather something passed to me in the MacAulay blood. There is no other way to explain it. I don't always love my brothers and sisters; in fact my Jack Russells, Tina and Sketch, have brought me more joy and earned more trust from me than many people I've met.

But that does not mean I am not there to protect them—each of them; every man, woman, and child who sleeps under my watch. It is akin to disagreeing with someone's opinion but being willing to die in order to defend their right to have and voice it.

I discovered a book a few months back—one written by Sean McCulloch. McCulloch had done extensive research into the major clans of Scotland. My own clan publicly died out in the early 18th century, however, the Book of Ossian clearly documents that this official removal of recognition of the MacAulay Clan was staged, in part, to divert attention from the covert actions of the clan to draw together a stronger force to wage a guerilla battle against the enemies of Ardincaple, Scotland, and the world at large.

9

I FIRST met Tilson Wayne in the forest south of Priest River. Amanda, Meyer, Jax, and I joined the search party the morning after investigating the crime scene at the Grant residence. The night had dumped eight inches of heavy rain across the countryside and it made trekking through the Idaho wilderness that much more difficult. The footing was treacherous at best, and the only shoes I'd brought for outdoor activity were my running shoes. My prosthesis was damn good handling semi-even terrain in the city, but the computer chip was finding the constant recalculations due to ever changing ground levels a bit challenging.

Overcompensation was the worst. I would be hiking up a steep embankment, the gyro having auto-adjusted to compensate for the additional force of the good climbing leg—then the incline would flatten for a moment, or dip in the other direction, and the leg would adjust too quickly, giving me the momentary sensation of having stepped for a stair in the dark that was not there—and I would go down, hard.

"Are you all right?" Amanda asked me after one such fall.

"Shit," I said. "Yeah. My ego took the brunt of it, I think."

"Let's rest," she said.

"Just me. You keep moving. I need a couple moments to adjust the calibration of this damn leg."

"You sure?"

"Yep. Head out."

Amanda left to catch up with Jax and Meyer. I unbuttoned my jeans, pulled them down, and opened up the module on my leg. I switched to manual stance calibration, which meant the artificial leg would be counting on me—what was left of my upper leg—to make the physical compensations. It was a lot more work, and made me slower and less wieldy, but the change would lessen the risk of going down again.

After putting my jeans back on, I caught movement out in the peripheral forest. I spun to see a man, maybe twenty feet away, standing still, his gaze locked on me. He then raised a hand in salutation. Another searcher, I assumed. I waved in return and he moved through the thick scrub, toward where I stood.

"Tilson Wayne," he said, extending a slender, nearly fleshless hand.

He was haggard and rough looking, a cigarette dangling from his lips. The majority of the left side of his face was tattooed with a strange design—almost like a Scot's war paint. His hair was stringy and full of grease, as if he'd never washed it.

I accepted his grip. His hand was as cold as the bottom of a grave.

"Sorry," he said. "Left my gloves in the truck."

"Bobby Mac," I said.

"I know. Word moves like greased pig shit in this little burg."

"Didn't see you at the gathering point this morning," I said.

"Don't care much for groups. Figured I would take a walk, see for myself what a man might find out here."

"No law against it, I suppose."

"Laws are for the innocent," he said, looking into the brooding sky. "Going to pound us here in a bit."

"What's your story, Mr. Wayne?"

"Tilly. Can't abide a man calls me by my father's name."

"Roger that."

"An asshole like no other you've ever encountered. Dear old dad, that is. You were in the Marines."

"You say that as a matter of fact, Tilly."

"It a fact or ain't it?"

"It's a fact."

"Then I stated correctly."

"Why am I getting the impression there's a little ass-busting going on here?" I said, sounding more perturbed than I was.

"A mountain man like me decides to bust your ass, you'll know it. Sorry for the directness. Afraid it's the only inheritance I received."

"Direct I can handle. Did you serve?"

"Never believed much in serving the innocent."

"That's twice you referenced the innocent. I take it that puts you in the guilty category."

"We're all guilty of something," Wayne said. "The innocent most of all."

"I happen to believe something pretty similar."

Tilson Wayne had distinguishing features—pointy chin with a long tuft of goatee and month-old facial hair. Big sideburns. Up close, the tattoo appeared to be a strange maze-like design. The skin on his face was sunbaked and leathery.

"Do you know the truth behind men such as us, Bobby?"

"Not sure we are cut from the same mold, sir."

"Family is everything."

"Family's not something we choose."

"Too often it don't choose us either."

"Almost never," I agreed.

"BOBBY," Amanda shouted from far up the trail.

"Here," I yelled back. She came jogging back into the small clearing where she'd left me.

"What the hell are you doing back here?" she said. "I had to double back something terrible."

"Sorry. Just chewing the rag with my new friend."

I turned around. Tilson Wayne had evaporated into the damp woodland air. Before Amanda could ask me what the hell I was talking about, a thunderhead broke and the heavens poured down unmercifully.

~ ~ ~

"Never heard of him," Jax told me in the police Suburban.

"Well I'm not crazy," I said, realizing how totally crazy it sounded to deny it. "You didn't see *anyone*?"

"No," Amanda said. "And you weren't exactly hidden from view either."

"Thanks."

"Just calling it like I see it. Or like I didn't see it."

"He said something about his old man. You know *any* Wayne's around here?"

"None currently," Jax said, "We can check county records when we get back."

We did just that. And there was one Wayne family listed in the census records.

"Percival Wayne," Jax said. "Looks like he and the wife died fifty years ago. No children."

"That's it?"

"That's it."

"Where are birth and death records?" Amanda said.

"Why?" Jax said.

"Census records that far back would have included a house count only. Any children who were born or died between counts wouldn't show up in the census reports."

"I need to hook you up with Marta Esteban. County Clerk. Woman is like a bloodhound when it comes to finding a needle in a pile of dusty records."

~ ~ ~

Marta Esteban was a pleasantly thick, onyx-haired, attractive mixture of Nez Perce and Latina and had the spunk to back it up.

"Bobby Macaulay," she said when we met her at the Records Division. "Your brother is a hunk and a half. Looks like you got a fair share of those genes, too."

I smiled in spite of myself. I don't think Amanda was amused, but she held her temper in check.

"We're looking for names," I said. "Babies that were born, died, anything with the Wayne surname."

"Done, Cariño. Your brother called ahead of you. I already have what you are looking for. Question is how much do you have in recompense."

"Barter, eh?" I said.

"Si, Cariño." Marta winked at me and Amanda kicked me in the shin for my part in the flirtation.

"I'm Amanda," she said. "Mother of the cariño's

child."

"Lo siento, Chiquita. No offense intended."

"You said you have some information for us?"

"Si, there was a baby born. 1922. 'Tilson'. Born to parents Percival and Agnes Wayne."

"Do you have any idea why the census would have missed this name?" I said.

"Census count back then was every fifteen years. There was a count in 1920 and again in 1935."

"Tilson was born and then died in-between."

"Si. There is a death certificate from 1933."

"Thank you, Marta," I said. "Jax is right, you're a star."

"There's more," she said. "I searched the old microfiche archives. We have articles from the *Coeur d'Alene Press* from everything after 1901. Including obituaries. Tilson Wayne died of injuries received in a farm accident. I printed the article for you."

"You're a doll, Marta."

She looked at Amanda and shrugged her shoulders. "If you get tired of him, or have any trouble putting him in his place, you know where to find me, Chiquita."

"Thanks," Amanda said. "For everything."

"Still think I was seeing things?" I said.

"No," Amanda said, holding the printout of the old article. "I didn't think you were crazy in the first place."

"I don't know. If we hadn't been at Grand Lake—if we hadn't witnessed the…well, you know. I don't know what I would believe. I certainly wouldn't blame anyone for thinking that."

"Why would Tilson Wayne be here now? And why

would he appear as the full-grown man you describe? Why would he appear only to you?"

"Hmm. Questions without answers. I think that's what they pay *us* for."

"We're going back to the search in the morning," she said.

"I think we need to talk to Meyer. The man with the plan. Have you seen him since we got rained out at the search?"

"He hitched a ride back with one of the deputies. Salem. Or Salon. Something like that. Said he had some research he wanted to do."

Meyer's room was three down from ours. He knew about my supposed meeting with Tilson in the forest but he'd not seen the newspaper article yet. It was time to share the knowledge.

I knocked on Meyer's door but there was no answer.

"He's not here," I told Amanda.

"Try his cell phone," she said.

"Cell phone? Ah, no. The man lives in the eighth century technologically speaking."

"There's really only one place where a technologically-challenged bibliophile in need of research would go."

"Public library."

"Viva la Dewey Decimal."

"You need to work on your Spanish. That might be exciting later on."

"Let's go, Cariño."

~ ~ ~

We found Meyer burrowed down in a cubical in the

darkest corner of the town library, surrounded by a stack of books three feet high. Two or three were opened in front of him. His eyes were blood red.

"Did you know this area was settled by French Canadian trappers and miners?"

"Jax mentioned something about that. Hadn't thought much about it," I said. "But *Coeur d'Alene* doesn't conjure images of a Germanic settlement."

"I found a reference," he said. "To bête noire."

"Black beast," I said. "Same as Father Terrence's journal."

"Yes and no. Same reference, the literal translation anyway. Turns out, however, *bête noire is* more appropriately used as a term of extreme anathema. I—it references the cursed. Or the damned."

"I'm assuming there is more."

"Indeed," Meyer said. "The early Native Americans met here by the French were called *Coeur d'Alene* by the trappers, in reference to their shrewd trading practices. The name's reference is believed to be *heart of the awl*, or *shrewd-hearted*. The Coeur d'Alene Indians believed in a beast—the creature of nek'we' aldarench, or 'one moon'—an evil presence that stalked pre-teen children for sacrifice to the evil God *Hamaltmsh*, loosely translated *fly god*."

"Loosely translated?" I said.

"The Coeur d'Alene language was almost exclusively spoken, not written. So textual references are a bit spotty. Most importantly, this creature stalked under the "one moon". Every two to three years, there is an *extra* full moon. A second full moon in what we know as our calendar month."

"A blue moon," Amanda said.

"Yes. The Coeur d'Alene called it 'one moon'. The Clergy used to refer to an extra moon as a 'belewe' or 'betrayer' moon."

"And the beast stalks during this time…this one moon?" I said.

"According to legend," Meyer said. "The sacrifice occurs on the one night of the nek'we aldarench."

"When is the next *one moon?*"

"October thirtieth."

"That's the day after tomorrow," I said.

~ ~ ~

The Scottish temper, at least as I know it, is a very real thing. It may also be the stuff of legends—portrayed as almost cartoonish at times; the brunt of jokes and funny sketches—but I can attest to its authenticity. There are times when there is absolutely nothing one can do about controlling it—particularly the one who is afflicted—and one might as well give in to the ride.

Such hotheadedness did not make the Macaulay relationships any easier to maintain.

Jax had invited Meyer, Amanda, and me out to his ranch for breakfast. Afterward we planned to join the search parties. There was no new information, and the rank and file of the volunteers were beginning to crack under the stress of knowing a young child could have been exposed to the elements (and God knew what else) for almost eight days. Additionally, the search parties had little more to go on than the day they began the search.

The Macaulay ranch is forty acres of property a few miles outside the town limits, nestled in a wooded valley with a roaring stream running through the middle of the land, providing plentiful, natural irrigation. It's really a gorgeous location.

Part of the reason for the size is the fact that my brother and his family raise suri alpacas. Now I can barely keep my domesticated canines fed and watered (and I've never been able to keep a plant alive for more than a few days at best), so I've never understood how a member of my family ended up raising *anything*, much less a herd of docile beasts that looked no different to me from llamas.

Apparently the business was very lucrative. Trish, Jax's wife of eighteen years, managed the bulk of the selling, purchasing, and breeding of the smelly animals. There was a single springtime fleecing each year, a big event whereby other members of the community traveled to the Macaulay ranch to help with the shearing (I do not know if they roped the alpacas, or drugged them—honestly I did not care to know the details). Trish also handled the business finances, so I really didn't think my brother had all that much to do with the ugly beasts. I made the mistake of telling him so while he grilled breakfast burritos on the back deck.

"How's Trish's business doing? Still a lot of money in smelly llama fur?" I said, playfully.

"You know damn well it's *our* business. And they're not llamas."

"But the fur still stinks something fierce, you have to admit."

"Are you picking a fight, or simply brewing one in your own mind?" Jax said.

"Ah, whatever, Jax. I've never witnessed you lift a finger to care for those beasts out there in the pasture. If your manhood is threatened by the woman in your life making a go of your business, I apologize."

The punch came from way low, him still holding the wooden handle of the spatula as his fist split my lip. I reacted, wrapping the crook of my elbow around his neck, locked it, and rolled, surprising him with the leverage. We went to the ground together, but I had the advantage. For the moment.

I kept the headlock and punched him with my other fist. Three times, four. We'd fought like this many times in our youth (and even a few times in adulthood) and I knew when he broke free—and he *would* break free—his size and considerable abilities would outmatch me. He knew me too well.

Trish came rushing through the French doors, yelling for us to stop.

I quit punching but did not release my brother. He was still far too pissed off, as was I.

"Call it off," I said through gritted teeth.

"Fuck you," Jax said.

"Call it off before your girls get out here and see us."

"Jackson, please," Trish said. "Stop this."

Jax put his arms out to his sides. "Done," he said. "Get the fuck off me."

I let go and rolled away, climbing quickly to my feet.

Jax stood slowly, wiping blood from his broken nose. "Jesus, you punch like a fucking *girl.*"

"Had to get my licks in quick."

"Smart plan," he said. "Let's get the burritos off the grill before they burn."

~ ~ ~

We were eating when the call came in from the precinct. Jax took the phone into the family room and then ran back into the kitchen nook where we were putting down the delicious breakfast he'd mastered on the grill.

He looked as if the wind had been stolen from him.

"What?" I said to him.

"There are two more," he said.

"Two more what?" Meyer said, but I knew.

So did Amanda.

~ ~ ~

Sarah Jennings and Elise Porter, each approximately the same age as Melissa Grant, had disappeared, presumably in the middle of the night. Both sets of parents said their daughters went to bed at a normal hour, nothing out of the ordinary. No strange sounds, no dogs barking. Both alarmed houses had remained silent. No sign of forced entry.

In the morning, the girls' rooms were simply empty, beds made as if they'd never slept there. The Porter parents stated they had actually looked in on Elise before they went to bed themselves. According to them, she was sound asleep, under the covers. Marcia Jennings claimed her daughter's room was a mess the evening before. They found it spotless as well as empty the next morning.

Meyer went back to the hotel and Jax took Amanda and me to the first crime scene, at the Porter residence. The family lived what appeared to be a fairly common middleclass existence. Elise's room was exactly as described; it did not look much like a place of abduction.

Nothing was disturbed, there were no tracks, and I doubted the forensic investigators were going to find any useful prints or DNA.

Too clean.

I put on latex gloves and looked through the trash can, under the sheets and pillows, beneath the bed. Nothing.

"Here's something," Amanda said from the other side of the room. Between her gloved index and middle fingers was a folded piece of paper.

"This was in one of the girl's tennis shoes," she said.

Amanda unfolded the paper to reveal a drawing of a symbol in the middle of the page. Jax and I examined the drawing.

"Seems too detailed for a child," I said.

"Maybe," said Jax. "Unser, get John Porter…he was

downstairs in the study."

When the deputy had retrieved Elise Porter's father Jax asked him:

"Have you seen this drawing before?"

"No. Where did you find it?"

"It was in her closet, in a shoe."

"Elise doesn't draw. I've never even seen her doodle."

Thanks, John." Jax motioned to Unser and the deputy walked John Porter from his daughter's room.

"Bag this," he told a member of the CSI team. His cell rang.

"Chief Macaulay."

After a few unintelligible grunts, he disconnected the call.

"CSI team found another drawing. This one is of a man."

"In Sarah Jennings' room," I said.

Jax nodded.

~ ~ ~

"Things like this just don't happen in my town," Jax said, driving us through the backstreets of Rocky Gap.

"Guessing they don't happen most places," I said.

"The Bureau has an excellent Behavioral Science Division," Amanda said. "The drawings may be able to tell us something."

"Don't need any feds to put their snouts in this investigation. Not yet, anyway," Jax said.

"I understand," said Amanda. "Feds have access to resources that may not be available here, is all I am suggesting."

"Here being in a dipshit town, you mean."

"No. Here being anywhere without access to the resources of the Federal Bureau of Investigation."

"Quit pissing across each other's bow," I said. "Let's see what this other drawing looks like. Jax, no one ever found anything like this at the Grant residence, did they?"

Jax shook his head. "Nothing."

"What about in the father's possessions?"

"Spence Grant's belongings? We confiscated a number of personal files. Don't think they've been fully vetted yet."

"We need to get on that," I said.

Jax dialed his cell.

~ ~ ~

When we arrived at the Jennings house the CSI team had the drawing bagged. I removed it with gloved hands. The detail, like our other drawing, was incredible, and I could not stop staring at the face before me.

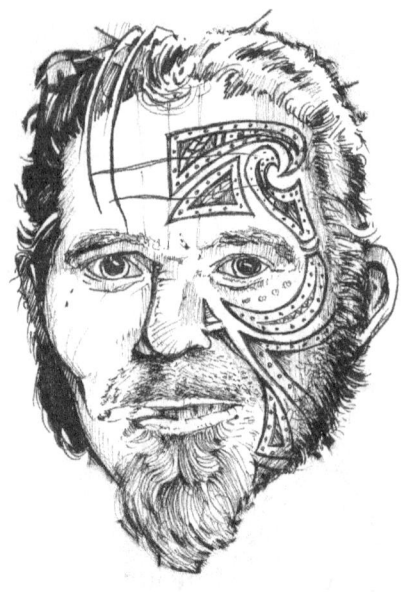

"That's Tilson Wayne."

~ ~ ~

FBI Field Agent in Charge Tanner Noon had waited for a case like this his entire career. Movement up and down the ladder in the Bureau was largely based on the cases an agent worked—and more importantly, the cases *solved.* Being reassigned to the Coeur d'Alene field office just five years out of Quantico should have been the death blow to Noon's career. It nearly was. Nothing ever happened in the panhandle of Idaho. There hadn't been a bank robbery in almost seventy years. The best Noon could hope for was a heist at one of the casinos on the reservation.

When the double-homicide was reported in Rocky Gap, Noon's spine had literally tingled. The town was definitely within his federal jurisdiction, but a homicide—even two of them—did not make a federal case. However, the Grant girl was *missing*. That suggested the possibility of a kidnapping, which was a federal crime. Chief of Police Jax Macaulay had been able to hold off Noon and his agents under the auspices that they didn't actually *know* young Melissa Grant had been abducted.

Not yet, anyway.

So the FBI didn't have a play in the case. As soon as they established that Melissa Grant was kidnapped, Noon could step in. He had no idea how long that might take—his orders were clear: maintain the professional relationship with local law enforcement. Which meant respecting the pace of their investigation, as frustrating as that pace might seem to an anxious agent wanting desperately to make a new name for himself.

Then the gods smiled down on Noon. Special Agent Amanda Byrne decided to give the Coeur d'Alene field office a call. Noon had no idea what Byrne was doing this far west and north; she was assigned to the coveted New York office.

"Agent Noon?"

"Yes. How are you, Amanda?"

"Fine, sir. I'm just north of you, in Rocky Gap."

"Official business?"

"Not exactly, sir."

"Call me Tanner."

Noon was hurt. Clearly Byrne didn't remember him, a fact that perplexed him nearly as much as it stung his pride. They went through Quantico together. That he outranked her was purely technical—a matter of a few extra months on the job. Noon had become an agent right after the academy where Amanda first participated in a certification class for elite marksmen.

"I know you're aware of the missing girl here," Amanda said.

"I am."

"They're in over their heads up here, sir."

"Unfortunately it's more complicated than that."

"I understand. That's why I'm calling."

"Obviously the Bureau would love to assist. We haven't got jurisdiction over the homicides, however, and so far our help hasn't been requested."

"Can I speak off the record?"

"Go ahead," Noon said.

"There have been two more abductions."

"Jesus."

"Jax Macaulay is sitting on the evidence. He obviously wants to solve this thing locally, but in my opinion, sir, that isn't going to happen."

"I can't move until I have something official. You know that. A police report. Something."

"Give me your fax number," Amanda said.

Ten minutes after the phone call with Agent Byrne ended, the documents he needed came through on the fax. Police reports detailing the three abductions, including a phone call from the first victim.

Tanner Noon called his superiors in Boise, who then called their superiors in Washington. The official report was a triple kidnapping in Rocky Gap, Idaho. Noon smiled deliciously. His superiors approved three helicopters out of Boise and a hundred field agents from regional and national offices. The contingency would fall under *his* command—it was agency protocol, but to Tanner Noon it was a life raft tossed into the pond he'd been drowning in for the past several years.

The army of agents would be arriving by the next morning and Noon would then storm northward to Rocky Gap. He couldn't wait to see the look on Jax Macaulay's face, the arrogant prick. He would decide later whether or not Chief Macaulay would face federal obstruction of justice charges.

~ ~ ~

"You did *what*?" I said when Amanda shared her phone call with the Coeur d'Alene office of the FBI.

"I had to. There wasn't a choice."

"It's you who is so fond of telling me there's *always* a choice."

"You're right. The choice I made was the necessary one. Those girls need every resource available."

"Didn't you think talking to me might be a good thing?"

"I knew what you'd say. And I have my duty, just like you. Nothing is getting done here, and it's my opinion your brother is in over his head."

"And me, too, is what you didn't say."

"I didn't say it because I don't believe it. But you aren't exactly running the investigation here, Bobby."

"What does that mean?"

"I don't want to fight about this. I know how things are with your brother. I think half the reason he called you up here was so that you could watch him solve the case."

"And save the day," I said.

"Exactly."

I knew she was right. Jax *was* in over his head. In fact, had the investigation been mine, I would have conceded that federal resources would only help. If Jax had included the FBI agents in Coeur d'Alene early on he likely could have avoided a jurisdictional pissing contest. As it stood, I was pretty certain we'd have seventy-five FBI agents here by morning and there would not be any question about who was running the show.

It still angered me that Amanda had not given me the respect of knowing what she planned to do before she actually did it.

"Look," I said. "I understand. Jax needs to prove himself. Always has. To me, to his superiors, to everyone. He's a good fucking cop, though. He and I both deserved more than an end around."

"I'm sorry," she said. "Seriously. I hope you see my reasoning, though."

"Next time, talk to me. You need to trust me."

"I *do* trust you. I just didn't want to put you in a position where you had to circumvent your brother. This way, it's on me."

"Fair enough," I said.

"How do we tell Jax?"

"I notice now that it's time to tell Jax, it's back to 'we'."

"Funny."

"We *both* tell him. I'll call him and see if he's at the precinct or at home."

~ ~ ~

We met Jax at his office. He'd slept there the night before, though he looked as if he had not rested in days. His face was drawn and covered in scraggly growth. There were bags under both bloodshot eyes.

We were both worried about how hard he was going to take the news about Tanner Noon and the swarm of FBI agents that were no doubt already assembling to crush my brother's hopes to save the town he'd sworn to protect. I would have felt similarly. Sometimes the logic of a decision is still not enough to assuage the wounding of its audacity. It's human nature; no one wants to be told he's not good enough for the task.

Least of all, my brother.

Jax sat in stony silence after Amanda described the phone call to him. Honestly, I'd never seen him react this way. His face was a natural color of pink, not red. His breathing was regular. He stared down some benign thought.

"How many?" is all he said.

"A hundred agents. Three choppers," Amanda said.

"The air support and the extra bodies will be a huge help," Jax said.

"A dozen of the agents have training in rough terrain tracking. Another two dozen are experts in kidnappings, abductions, whatever. Point is they will be bringing a lot of talent to bear on this situation."

"I get it," he said.

"Look, Jax..." I said, but he stifled me with a palm pressed to the air.

"We're going to need a better command post," Jax

said.

Amanda looked at me and I nodded.

"They're bringing their own," she said.

"Of course they are."

10

THE SHEER show of FBI force was impressive. I'd seen it a few times before in Denver, and though most local cops would never admit it, the feds really did have all the resources and when they mobilized, it was worth stopping to stare. Blue jackets with **FBI** emblazoned brashly across the middle of the back in stark yellow contrast; two large motor homes converted into state of the art command centers, painted pearl black, with opaque, bulletproof windows; three government issued helicopters with three crack pilots.

I only hoped the arsenal would help us get those three girls back. There comes a point when territorial behavior needs to sit down, shut up, and allow common sense to take over. We had three missing eleven-year-old girls and the unspoken concern was that these might not be the last of them. After all, we couldn't protect every household, every bedroom, and every eleven-year-old girl in the county. Not even the FBI could accomplish that—but with numbers like those, it was a fine start.

"Tanner Noon," the agent in charge said, introducing himself to the collective of Jax, Amanda, and myself.

"Special Agent Amanda Byrne. We spoke on the phone."

"You don't remember me, Agent?"

"Sir?"

"We attended Quantico together. You turned down

83

my advances more times than I care to recount."

"The bad crew cut," Amanda said, smiling.

"I was young. Trying to save a buck."

"Good to see you again, sir."

"Tanner, please. Introduce me to your friends."

"Chief Jackson Macaulay," Jax interjected before Amanda could do it for him. "We've spoken also."

"I recognize the voice," Noon said, extending five manicured nails and a hand to go with them. "Sorry for the intrusion."

"Yeah," Jax said, and shook Noon's hand as limply as I'd ever seen him.

"You must be the detective from Denver," he said. He didn't offer his hand to me. Apparently I was in the wrong pond. Or with the wrong girl. I couldn't yet decide which.

"Bobby Macaulay. Mac is fine."

"All right then," Noon said. "Join me in Command One for a briefing?"

~ ~ ~

If the command vehicles looked impressive from the outside, they were pure technological genius on the interior. Not one inch was underutilized. I had to give the federales credit: this was no vacation home, filled with overpriced creature comforts. They'd flown them in to Lewiston-Nez Pearce County Airport on a C-5 Galaxy transport plane, along with a dozen SUVs and the army of agents that had turned the trailhead into a staging ground the size of two football fields.

Agent Noon had a digitized map up on one of the big

screens. Using a special pen on the tabletop computer in front of him, he drew lines on the map that appeared simultaneously on the big screen on the wall.

"As we speak, the choppers are taking off to form a triangle and begin working this entire area in rotating pieces. Strict military sectioning. Once they've canvassed the entire area, if unsuccessful, they will repeat until we find something.

"It's all low altitude searches, with two spotters per bird. If a deer farts down there, we'll know it."

I glanced sideways at Amanda. She seemed all ears.

"I've got sixty agents divided into teams of a dozen. One tracker per team. That's five teams, forming a skirmish line and beginning at the southern end of the Coeur d'Alene boundary.

"We'll be working these woods, mountains, dells, valleys, riverbeds, and every other square inch of this godforsaken wilderness from dawn until dusk. We're going to find those little girls."

"Don't say that to the parents," Jax said. "Or the media. Don't you ever tell them we are going to find them. You tell them you're doing everything you can. That's it."

"Easy, Chief. Just an expression. I know how to handle the press."

"And the families."

"What?"

"I said, 'and the families'."

"Right, yes, the families as well."

"Where do we fit in all this," Jax asked.

"You?"

"My department. My brother. Agent Byrne. Do you need a digitized map, Agent?"

"Tanner. I told you all to call me Tanner."

"Do you?"

"Do I what?"

"Do you need a map, Noon? What do you need us doing?"

"I don't need you doing anything," Noon said. "What I am directing you to do is remain in town—at the precinct, at the local donut shop, I don't really give a shit, Chief. Just stay out of the way. Your brother is away from home, and I'm not exactly sure what Agent Byrne is doing up here. As a matter of fact, Amanda, you are more than welcome to assist us up here, in an official capacity, I mean."

"I'd like that," she said. "I need to go to town, get my gun, etcetera. Back later in the afternoon?"

"Perfect," Noon said, and looked at us collectively. "Thank you for taking the time, gentlemen. Please excuse me."

~ ~ ~

The three of us rode back to the Rocky Gap precinct in silence. I knew why Amanda had agreed to Noon's offer, or at least I thought I did. I admit I'm not much good handling the green-eyed beast of jealousy. Particularly when the perceived threat comes from one as politically-motivated as Agent Tanner Noon. I had to admit, his plans were flawless and well-conceived. Other than his minor commentary before we left—one that was certainly brought about by my own brother's callused words—I had no procedural issue with the man.

Which is why I could not stop wondering how a

cocksure agent like Noon somehow got himself assigned to the smallest outpost south of the Arctic Circle.

"Are you going to talk to me," Amanda whispered in my brother's office while he was out filling his coffee mug.

"Sorry," I said. "This whole FBI/Noon thing has me a bit perplexed."

"He's a good agent," she said. "But you know why I agreed to go back up there."

"I do."

"Then what's the problem, kind sir?"

"Nothing. He's a little too sure of himself, that's it."

"Everything seemed by the book. And Jax…"

"Jax got what he had coming. I have no truck with that."

"Good. Say goodbye to your brother for me. I need to get back to the command post. Hopefully we'll have some good things to talk about tonight."

"You realize you're going to be sworn to secrecy the moment you arrive?"

"Yet you have all the keys to my vault."

When the lady was right, she was right.

~ ~ ~

"Where's Amanda?" Jax said as he walked back in. "Returned to the fold?"

"Easy."

"Ah, hell, I knew damn well it was going to shake out like this. I only wanted to get in my parting shots. Can't exactly punch the guy, now can I?"

"No, probably not," I said, grinning a little.

It was the first time my brother had made me smile since we were kids. It felt good. Like old times.

"I want to lay out a theory I came up with last night."

"I take it this has nothing to do with a donut shop?"

"Nothing says we can't keep following up on leads, right?"

"Give it to me."

"Annir basically told us where to look, right?"

"Yeah."

"Why would he do that? I mean, assuming he didn't want to be found."

"His confidence could be as strong as he implied," I said.

"Maybe. But still, why give yourself away?"

"Look," I said. "These bad guys in Denver. That was their style. 'Fuck you. Come and get us' kind of mentality."

"Okay. But that was them."

"True enough. What are you thinking?"

"I've been thinking of the exact opposite of where we're all looking right now."

"Okay."

"The search is on in the middle of nowhere."

"Yep."

"Maybe the victims are here. In town. Closer than we could imagine."

"It's not a bad theory," I said. "I like it."

"And it gives us something to do while Wyatt Earp is busy blowing holes in the O.K. corral."

"I'm with you."

It made sense. And he was right about it giving us something to do. Not only was Noon looking for a gunfight up in the forest, I figured he also had designs on my woman. More than anything I needed something to occupy the brain.

~ ~ ~

We couldn't exactly go door to door. So Jax wanted to start in the least likely places first.

"Jennings or Porter residence," he asked.

"What about the Grants?"

"Less obvious than the Coeur d'Alene, more obvious than homes with parents still living in them."

"Flip a coin," I said.

"Nah, my gut says the Porter residence."

No destination is far in Rocky Gap. We were at the Porter's doorstep in less than five minutes. Jax rang the bell. No answer. He rang it again. Two vehicles were parked in the driveway, but still no answer.

He motioned to the side of the house and we walked around to the rear. No sounds, no movement. Nothing. There was a dog crate and a leash lying on the deck, but no barking.

I motioned to the canine paraphernalia and pointed to my ears. People could stay quiet. Dogs, not so much. We both drew our weapons. Jax motioned to me to circle the deck and come from the other side. He waited until I was in place and then we both climbed the stairs closest to the house, keeping our profiles small against the wood siding.

Before we could reach the sliding door, the back wall exploded. Glass, wood, wire, and insulation blew outward in a cloud and a handful of gnarled, blackish shapes, each twice our size, flew past us, running for the far end of the yard. We both leveled our pistols but were too late. The beasts were far too fast and had scaled the back fence and disappeared in less than a second or two.

"Jesus Christ," Jax breathed. Debris lay all about the grass and there was a jagged hole encompassing more than a third of the back of the house. "What the hell?"

I motioned to the house. There was a small whine coming from within. Deep within. We put our weapons back to the ready and slowly moved to the gaping tear in the Porter's home. After clearing the entrance, and the first two rooms we entered, Jax pointed to the basement stairs. The whimpering was clearly coming from down below.

I pointed to the rest of the house. We needed to make sure the first level was clear. Jax nodded and we made a quick sweep of the upstairs.

As we descended the stairs to the underground, I could now tell the sounds were coming from the dog. The unfinished basement was a mess. The things we'd seen had obviously been living down here. A Golden Retriever was lying in the corner, bleeding. It looked like the beasts had been playing with it, as the cat might play with the outmatched rodent rather than delivering a quick death.

"Sorry, girl," I said, scratching her ears. It didn't do any good. She was nonresponsive. The poor dog was well beyond anything being done to save her and was clearly in a massive amount of anguish. I knew what had to be done, but I could not bring myself to do it. Images of Tina and Sketch occupied my head. I knew I owed it to them, and to the animal at my feet, to relieve her suffering; it was my limitation, not hers. They do not ask much of us for their unequaled love and loyalty, but this one thing. And I was failing this poor dog.

Jax could see the indecision playing out on my face. He pointed to the mess strewn across the basement and told me to check the room for any signs of the victims having been here. When I turned to begin the search, he fired.

~ ~ ~

There were no signs of the girls, the Porters, or any other humans. I say humans; Jax was still not convinced we'd seen anything but several large brutes running for freedom.

"Squatters?" he said.

"Not a chance. Did you see the dog?"

"Sadistic squatters, then."

"And the Porters?"

"No answer for that one, I'm afraid," Jax said.

"I have one."

"See, I was afraid you were going to say that."

"You never really told me how much you heard about what went down in Denver."

"That's because I lied about how I heard about it."

"Do tell," I said.

"I dreamed it."

"Excuse me?"

"I'm not sure exactly whether it was before, after, or during what happened to you down there. But I dreamed it. Like the way twins talk about living events of the other, from a thousand miles away? That was me. Ask me anything."

"You sound pretty sure of yourself," I said.

"Can't explain that, either. But I know. Ask me."

"Calypso?"

"I saw him warn you away on that rooftop. Threatening to throw Cole off the building."

"Jesus."

"And Greer…"

"Shit."

"I know you had no choice. I know how much it killed you."

"Then what is all this crap about squatters?"

"Wishful thinking?"

The second smile in the same day.

"Those things," he said to me. "The Porters and the Jennings?"

"That's what I'm afraid of."

"This makes no sense," he said.

"I promise you, there is some reason for it."

"I'm all ears."

"Did the stories about the girls' abductions play funny for you?"

"Thoroughness of the disappearing act?"

"Exactly."

"So you're thinking the parents were in on it?"

"I'm thinking the parents weren't the parents. Not for a long time, even."

"So Annir got to them?"

"He got to Spence Grant…"

"We need to talk to him again."

~ ~ ~

Amanda remembered more about Agent Tanner Noon than she let on. In fact, she remembered each of his terribly sleazy advances at Quantico, and she'd also followed his unimpressive career within the Bureau. Noon could not be trusted. The last thing she wanted to do, however, was worry Mac. He was hip deep with his brother, and then there was the baby.

Amanda was a woman—nay, an *agent*—who could handle herself. So she played it up a little with Noon. Mac had a good head on his shoulders; he knew she was up to something, and a bit of jealousy could be a healthy thing.

"I'm glad you decided to come work with the pros," Noon said as they walked from Command One to the chow hut.

"I can only take local law enforcement for so long," she said. "I mean, Jax is a decent cop…it's just that there is only so much a local cop can get accomplished."

"Let it go, is what I always tell them."

"Yep. Gotta know when to fold the hand, sir."

"Tanner."

"Sure. Tanner. So what are the choppers seeing…anything?"

"Not so far. It's early, though. They need to familiarize with the terrain, the best hiding places. What's the story with you and Macaulay?"

"Bobby, you mean."

"Yeah, him. Tough guy, right?"

"He's a guy that can hold his own."

"How much of yours is he holding?"

God, the man made her skin go clammy and her stomach feel like a swarm of eels were swimming around inside her.

"See, Tanner. There you go with that charm that got you so far at the Academy."

"So you *do* remember me."

93

"I remember you hitting on me. I would have thought your tact improved with age."

"I'm still commanding officer here, you know."

"Can't have it both ways, slugger. It's Tanner or it's sir. I'm not going to play games. You respect me, I respect you. But if you're going to get off poking holes in Mac, you can take *Tanner* and shove it up your ass."

Nice. Well played, she thought sardonically.

"Whoa there, lady. Mea culpa, mea culpa. Didn't intend to ruffle feathers. Tanner will do."

What a spineless douche, Byrne thought. But it worked.

"Fine. Mac and I have worked together. And we see each other sometimes. Nothing exclusive."

"See," Noon said. "We can play nice."

"Fair enough," Byrne said.

Keep your fucking enemies close, is what she thought.

11

JAX CONDUCTED the second interview with Spence Grant. We both agreed that my presence would be a bad idea. Plus, if the County Attorney were to hear about me being allowed in the same room with the suspect again— well, that would be too much like building a fire next to a keg of black powder.

I stayed behind the one-way glass.

"We just got back from the Porter house," Jax said to Spence Grant.

"How are they? The Porters, I mean."

"Why would you think I meant anyone else?"

"No reason."

"I'd say the Porters have seen better times."

"Losing a daughter will do that to you."

"It goes beyond losing a daughter, what we saw."

"Have you heard the line 'each of us, a monster within'?" Spence said.

"I haven't."

"I think it was Dostoevsky. Or Merv Griffin."

"You have any ideas about what was happening over at the Porter house, Spence?"

"I have a few."

"I'd like to hear them."

"Bring your brother in here and I'll tell you."

"Not a great idea," Jax said. "You of all people should see that."

"I talk to the two of you or no one at all."

Jax came out and stood in front of me. I'd been listening to the whole exchange. He had an expression that said this is a really, really bad idea.

"I can be cool," I said.

"You need to be better than *cool*. Like ice water. Even cooler."

"Get under my skin twice, shame on me."

"Let's figure out what this turd knows."

"Detective Macaulay," Spence Grant said happily when we walked in, as if he'd known me all his life and had missed me terribly.

"Mr. Grant," I said.

"Come on, Mac...*Spence*. We can't talk if we aren't friends, am I right?"

"Spence, then."

"You all had quite an experience at the Porter house."

"What do you know about it," Jax asked.

"I know some. More than I want, as much as I need."

"We'd like to know about the Porters," I said. "When they were lost."

"One person's loss is another's gain," Spence said. He seemed fairly impressed with himself, and I realized the initial familiarity I had felt when we first met was gone. This guy was a horse's ass.

"When did Rule get to the Porters?" I said.

"It wasn't anyone named 'Rule'. It was Annir. Annir got to them. And to the Jennings."

"When?"

"Over a year ago."

"What?" Jax said.

"The parents of those girls have been gone for over a year," Spence said.

"Impossible," Jax said.

"Oh, it's possible. You'd be surprised at the makeup of your quiet little town here…not nearly as quiet as it used to be. Or more quiet. Depending on your perspective."

"This is crazy," Jax said.

"What's going on?" I said. "What's the end game?"

"End game…I like that," Spence said, his eyes twinkling. "Did you read *Ender's Game*, by Orson Scott Card, Mac?"

"No. Can't say I did."

"One of the all-time great Sci-Fi epics," he said. "Not unlike now, mankind is facing extinction at the hands of superior beings."

"Is that what's happening?" I said. "Do you believe we're facing extinction?"

"You're missing the point. These humans put their faith in the children."

"Children?"

"They're our future. They've always been our future. For better, for worse. Good or evil. You can't *have* a future without them. Without them, the future is LOST."

~ ~ ~

Spence Grant had little else to say. He was only giving up as much as required. Unfortunately, his allegiance was still clearly drawn.

Jax went home to be with his family and I went back to the hotel to attempt sleep. I desperately needed some rest. I immediately fell into a coma-like sleep, expelling all the stress of the past few days in one glorious release. It was in this deep sleep that Greer appeared to me, in all her splendor.

"Why are you up here, Bobby Mac?"

"You know why. Because I can't just let these things slide anymore. Not since…"

"Not since me?"

"That's part of it. I miss you, Greer."

"Problem is you didn't miss me enough when I was *alive*."

"I know."

"I miss you, too, Bobby."

"I wish you wouldn't say that."

"Because it hurts you too much."

"Yes."

"I did, you know."

"Did what?"

"I really did love you."

"I'm afraid that's my subconscious, telling me what I want to hear."

"Doesn't make it any less true."

"I'd give anything to believe that."

"You can believe it."

"Why come to me now? It's been over a year…"

"This place isn't safe."

"So you're here to warn me off?"

"Something like that."

"I can't do it, Greer. There's too much at stake."

"What about your nieces?"

"What about them?"

"What you need to be doing is saving them."

"How?"

"He wants them all."

"The children?"

"The girls."

And then I awoke. The phone was ringing.
It was Meyer.

~ ~ ~

I called Jax at his house.

"Are Gracie and Celia all right?"

"Yeah, I mean I think so," Jax said through the cobwebs. "Gracie is at her friend's place."

"Are you shitting me? With everything going on, Jax?"

"We have to live our lives. Gracie's fine."

"Get your daughter. I'm coming over."

By the time I arrived, Jax was on his second mug of coffee and Trish had gone to pick up Gracie at the friend's house.

"Hope this is good," Jax said.

"Meyer is on his way."

"Meyer."

"Yes."

"What's this about?"

"He found something," I said. "In the history books. Something about the children."

"The *children*?"

"Young girls. Are you familiar with *Three Sisters Peaks*?"

"Yeah, I think so. In the range overlooking Lake Pend Oreille."

Meyer burst into the room, sweaty and out of breath. He looked like he was about to drop. When Scots like Meyer become taxed, their fair skin turns tomato red and veins begin popping out where they were hidden before.

"Ease up, Meyer," I said.

"We need to gather all the people in town with kids,"

he said in-between breaths. "Especially young daughters."

"Jesus," said Jax. He snatched his cell from the table and dialed Trish.

"No answer," he said. "DAMN it."

"What did you find? Tell us," I said.

"It's in our own book. Can you believe it?"

"Calm down. What...did...you...find?"

"Sacrifice," he said. "I think they are trying to sacrifice three young girls."

"Mac said something about *sisters*," Jax said, almost pleading. "*Three Sisters Peaks.*"

"I think so," Meyer said. "The grouping of peaks was named from a ritual that occurred there a hundred and fifty years ago. A splinter of the Coeur d'Alene tribe. Witch doctors and warriors who believed the gods were angry with the white man—the French. They kidnapped three daughters of a French Captain...took one to each peak. And when the three fires were lit—when the signal was given between the three spires—the witch doctors threw the girls to their deaths."

"What does this have to do with us?"

"There was a similar action in the fifteenth century. In Scotland. Two warring clans. One clan captured three daughters of the opposing leader. Burned them at the stake to show their resolve."

"Their resolve to what?" I said.

"To end the lineage of their enemies."

"And you think Rule is somehow reenacting this ritual."

"I think Annir appeared as a god to the splintered tribe of Coeur d'Alene. Convinced them of the need for the sacrifices."

"You talked about this before, right?"

100

"Yes. He had a different name then: *Hamaltmsh*."

"The fly god."

~ ~ ~

Trish arrived with Gracie and Celia a few minutes later. Jax grabbed the girls, checking them over as if they might have been damaged on the Jeep ride over. He next called his lead deputy.

"Severs. Use the reverse 911 procedures. All citizens are to congregate in orderly fashion in the school sports complex—use the indoor football field; it's the largest. Put them in the gymnasium, too, if you have to. Round up everyone—County Sheriffs, too. Tell them it's on my authority. And Bill...*arm yourself*."

"We should call the FBI. Call Noon," I said.

"Agreed. From the school. Securing the town, that's first."

I nodded and looked to Meyer, who had dropped on a couch and looked better.

"What else do you know?"

"As I said, there is a reference to a similar act in the Book of Ossian. Three daughters. Sisters. It was meant to end the family line."

"When again?"

"The fifteenth century. The Clan MacDougal. Three young girls were captured by a marauding faction of an unknown clan. At the time the murders were believed to be politically motivated—the MacDougals were warring with several other clans and some of their nobles sided with the English. The poet who documented the event in the Book of Ossian believed otherwise."

"What?"

"He believed the girls were sacrificed before the demigod Samhain. A ritual to end the MacDougal lineage."

"Not a warring clan?"

"No. Demons."

"This is in the book?"

"Yes…and also this depiction of a symbol, carved into the dead girls' abdomens prior to the burning."

"Jesus," Jax said. "How do we know who to warn?"

"What is he talking about, Mac?"

"We've got our own disturbing news."

~ ~ ~

When they had gathered all the residents of Rocky Gap in the gymnasium and on the football field, Chief Jax Macaulay calmed their fears. He told them the evacuation of their homes was strictly precautionary; that the best way for him and his deputies to protect the families and children of their tightknit town was to have them all in one place.

"We don't need more disappearances," he said to the

people, most of whom he knew well; many whose sons and daughters played soccer with Gracie or with Celia on the playground. "What we can't afford is panic. We've got food and water here from Alton's Grocery, and Doc Carroll is here and can look at anyone who isn't feeling well."

There were questions, and Jax fielded them as well as he knew how.

No, he didn't know how long they would be there.

No, there wasn't any eminent danger to anyone.

Yes, the school would be closed in the morning.

For the most part, this demand of the job was easy. Compared, at least, to what he feared they might have to do later on—if their fears came to fruition, that was.

"People seem to be taking this in stride," I told him.

"Why shouldn't they? This is more excitement than most of them have seen their entire lives. Plus they have no idea what's going on. Ignorance is being fat, dumb, and oblivious."

"Have you called Noon yet? Amanda's not picking up."

"No. Figured I'd try now."

He dialed the number on the back of the business card Agent Noon gave him.

"I'm going outside to see if I can find Meyer," I said.

The night was aglow with the light from the waxing *one moon*. The only bodies outside were Sheriff and Police personnel. I nodded at Deputy Solon as I walked by her. She returned my nod nervously. Unlike the ordinary citizens, even though she did not know specifics, Solon knew there was a lot more to calling in every resident of a town than what Jax had let on.

Where the hell is Meyer, I thought. It was his normal

103

modus operandi—disappearing, leaving the group to wander in deep thought. Having spent most of his adult life as a priest, Meyer was as personable as required; he did not do well in large groups.

There was a shout from behind the school and a noise like trash cans falling over. I drew my nine and moved quickly in the direction of the commotion.

I found Meyer, lying in a pile of refuse, having stumbled into the trash cans. The man had night blindness; the incandescence of the near-full moon wasn't of much help to him.

I gave him my hand and pulled him up from the ground.

"You'd think I would learn," he said.

"You'd think *I* would," I told him.

"What, my friend, is *that* supposed to mean?"

"You test me. What are you doing back here?"

"Thinking."

"Can't you think inside the building? There are plenty of dark hallways."

"The night air calms my nerves."

"You are *night blind*."

"A limitation to which I am not yet willing to relinquish control," he said.

"You are as stubborn as me," I said.

"NO ONE is that stubborn."

"This might be one argument I'm forced to concede."

"You've never won an argument with me. I doubt you ever will."

"Stubborn and egotistical," I said. "Nice combination."

"There is something I'm missing."

"Things have gone so out of whack, I'd be shocked if

104

we *hadn't* missed something."

"What I mean is, I've read hundreds of books this past week—yet my theories feel weak. Unsubstantiated."

"So far you're the one who has figured all of this out. Without your theories, we wouldn't know anything at all."

He contemplated this for a moment before answering me.

"Let me rephrase: I feel more like I have put together a puzzle, and we can indeed see what we are dealing with, but there are pieces missing. Perhaps critical pieces."

"What more can you do?"

"I can go back to my studies. You are the doer. I am the thinker. We complement each other."

"I'll take that in the positive light in which I know it was offered."

"Please do," Meyer said. "And then drive me back to the library."

"The library will be closed."

He smiled. "There are ways around such things."

R.S. GUTHRIE

12

THE THING Bobby Macaulay knew as Father Rule surveyed the legions his servant Annir had gathered for the attack. Rule had known many such subservient allies through the millennia, but none quite as eager and decent at his work as Annir. Truly one of the only creatures in the realm that cared not for praise or status or reward. Annir wanted to spill blood; he wanted to embody *evil*.

A Celt warrior of one kind or another, Rule had easily converted him. Converting the weak was one thing, but when a human exhibited such raw desire and aptitude for the taking of life, Rule's job was as fulfilling as it was simplified.

All things had gone according to plan. Rule enjoyed the chess match; he relished each move, even when a thousand years between one and the next. The demon's arrogance made the game more difficult to enjoy—so sure he was of his eventual victory. There was, however, no preordained outcome—much as Rule would have welcomed such reality. The Universe did not work that way. This war would last for infinity.

"It's time," Rule said to Annir. "They are not to return until it's finished."

Annir hobbled down from the precipice, joining the throng of black, spiny, hateful things. He walked among them, his thoughts permeated their dark consciousness, telling them to kill everyone—leave no one alive except the three.

Go. Destroy.

There were thousands. Far too many for those who would fight them below. Every manner of soulless creature from beyond the borders of Hell had been summoned. None resembled humans any longer. Column after column, row after row began to descend through the forest and toward the humans, picking up speed and beginning to howl with bloodlust. So rarely they were allowed to feed on humans, the fever enveloped them.

No tree or rock or hillside was left undamaged in their wake. The humans were not far, congregated below, resting, waiting for who knew what. Sitting ducks, Annir thought hungrily. Pigs awaiting the slaughter.

~ ~ ~

Byrne heard the demons before anyone else. How could she not have? She knew the sound; she remembered the terrifying cries from the wilderness in Colorado. Those inhuman screams still lived in her nightmares.

The hundred or so FBI agents had pulled back from the search in anticipation of nightfall. The choppers had landed and the pilots, agents, and other technical personnel were busy gorging themselves in the chow tent, laughing, joking, and telling stories of heroism—wagging their braggadocio for all to see.

So glib, Amanda had thought, just moments before. So nonchalant and carefree while there were still three young girls missing in the inhospitable Idaho wilderness.

Amanda pulled her sidearm and shouted "READY."

Only a handful of agents responded, their training overriding any questions or confusion. The rest either stopped talking, wondering what the female agent was doing, or paid her no mind at all.

They would pay attention soon enough. The howling had grown to a kind of raging white noise. Soon all the agents began looking around, wondering from where the noise emanated. Two dozen more un-holstered their weapons.

The ground beneath the tent began shaking as the thundering herd came down the mountainside. In the shocked silence of the mess hall, the sounds of trees cracking apart and the now frenzied shrieks could be clearly heard.

There was a sudden explosion as the generators near the outskirts of camp were destroyed. The lights went out and the inside of the tent became pandemonium. Agents bounced off one another in panic, pulling their side arms, searching for automatic rifles, knives, anything that could be used against whatever approached.

Then the first of the demons arrived. Those first attackers tore through the outer walls and poured into the crowded tent. The room was completely shrouded in darkness, but the sounds of automatic and semi-automatic gunfire erupted on all sides of Amanda, pounding her eardrums and drowning out the sounds of the crazed demons.

Amanda tried to move to the center of the room, away from the edges of the attack where men and women were being decimated. The sounds of dying could be heard above the sound of gunfire. The stench of burnt cordite and fresh blood filled the air.

Agent Byrne pulled as many agents close to her as she could and they formed a small phalanx, weapons drawn, pointed outward, ready to fire. Amanda's stomach tossed like a trapped animal inside her. She understood what they were up against; she knew the odds were worse than poor. They had to be outnumbered ten to one. Their enemy thrived in darkness, dwarfed them in numbers, and had an insatiable hunger for human life.

"Stay together," she told those closest to her. "Remember your training. Put the rest out of your mind."

The latter was not an easy command. They were losing the battle—inch-by-inch, moment-by-moment, death-by-death. The gunfire was lessening by orders of magnitude as wave upon wave of attackers slowly overcame what nominal resistance the humans could muster.

When the first cluster of gnarled, misshapen bodies reached Amanda and her comrades, she called for the agents to fire their guns. Short bursts. Shooting to kill.

It didn't take long.

They would have run out of ammunition eventually anyway, but the onslaught of demons was by then far too much for a handful of agents to stave off, even for a few minutes.

When it was over, every agent around her was eviscerated. Torn, mangled, and devoured. Bones crunched about her as if they were nothing more than twigs and toothpicks. And when they were done with the savage killing, the knot of creatures encircled her.

She was prepared to die. Her training had ingrained such a possibility into her psyche. What she found herself unready to face was the destruction of the life inside her. There was no manual, no amount of rote that could make her ready to accept that.

But she'd finally run out of choices.

Her last thoughts were of Bobby Mac and the children they would never have.

Part II

LOST

R.S. GUTHRIE

13

PEOPLE BECOME lost in many different ways. I have discovered this reality over half a lifetime. Each of us figures it out eventually. It happens differently for every person, but there are similarities.

Sometimes, after having once been certain of our path and making progress toward what we believed to be our future, something happens. A life-changing event. This unthinkable happening then acts as a detour, sending us down an unfamiliar path. Once we've walked far enough down into the realm of the unknown, our ability to find the way back to the main route is forever lost.

We can also experience a much more subtle sense of loss. It is possible to simply wake up one morning like a man or woman with amnesia. Our life looks differently than when we drifted off to sleep. Unrecognizable. Unfathomable. How did we get to this place in our lives? Some call this mid-life crisis. Others, an epiphany or an awakening.

Another way we lose our bearings is by having too much taken away. An avalanche of tragedy can leave us bewildered, disoriented, trepid toward a step in any direction. We feel as if the immediate area is filled with landmines, tripwires, pitfalls—no way seems safe to traverse.

And it is then we stay frozen. The only action that

feels safe is no action at all. We crawl within ourselves, sometimes for years. By refusing to make any choices—by ceasing to act—we believe we are ridding ourselves of all risk.

For me, it was none of the above. Or all of them, combined as one. For me, it was like finding yourself in a nightmare and not being able to coax the mind awake. No matter what you do, you can't wake up—but neither can you shake the surreal feeling that this is *not your life*. Eventually you realize you are not asleep, but that you'd rather you were. Instead, you are faced with a living nightmare.

The scene at the staging ground was beyond what I could have possibly imagined. When we could not reach Amanda, Noon, or any other agents, we of course knew something was wrong. It was far worse than that. I have seen war. As a Marine, I served in Iraq during Desert Storm, just at the end of my enlistment. And although we did not encounter a large resistance, I saw firsthand what a monster does to his own people. Mass graves, the aftermath of death squads. But I was wrong. That was what a dictator did to his people. Spread before us, there at the staging ground, was the aftermath of true monsters.

It could not be said that we found bodies; *bodies* implies a measure of continuity or of noticeable form. There was no continuity or form in the total devastation before our eyes. It would take months—perhaps *years*—to identify what body parts were intact enough for a forensic team to *attempt* an examination.

I was not there at Ground Zero in New York. I have friends in the Denver Fire Department who were called out. I have read many of the accounts. I can only imagine it resembled the carnage that Rule's demons had inflicted upon the poor souls who were here.

And I knew what this all meant to me, on a personal level.

It was hard to even think her name.

Amanda.

And our child.

"My God," Jax said, his face pallid and bereft of emotion.

I couldn't speak. There were no words. The wellspring of pain was pressing on my sternum, begging release. It felt as if I might crumble inward. Cease to exist.

"She's gone," I finally managed.

"We don't know that."

"Look at this carnage. Look at what they did. Nothing survived. This was meant as an extermination."

More like a *holocaust.*

"I need to call in the State Police," he managed.

"Call them," I said and walked away.

In the trees, I searched for solitude. I needed to separate from the awful silence resounding from my own soul. Never had I felt so empty; so without purpose. What was left? What could I possibly find now worth going on toward?

"You have your son," a voice from behind me said.

I spun around.

It was Tilson Wayne, sitting on a broken tree, smoking a hand-rolled cigarette. The coal glowed orange-red in the damp darkness.

"Where the fuck did you come from?" I hissed. "Were you are part of this?"

"Of course not," he said.

"Why are you here now?"

"You know why."

"No riddles. Not now. Just talk to me. I need to hear *something*."

"It's not over," he said.

I was once again entranced by his rough, leathery features. So much history in those lines and scarred skin—too much for a man who died as a child.

"It doesn't get much more 'over' than this."

"There's more to come."

"That's not reassuring."

"Giving up is not in your nature," he said.

"How the hell do you know anything about my nature?"

"You know the answer to that one, too," he said, and drew smoke deep into his lungs.

"You aren't even real. Go away. I'll suffer the silence."

"You know how the game is played. There isn't an end, Bobby. There never will be."

"Like I said, no riddles, ghost. Evaporate. Fly off. Whatever the fuck it is you do."

"Every act is a part of the grand plan. Even one as heinous as this."

"You're not making sense," I said.

"What have you learned about me?"

"About you?"

"My history."

"That you died as a child."

"I did."

"Yet here you are."

"I have no memory between then and now," he said.

"That's because you aren't real. You are something I dreamed up. More evidence that I'm going crazy."

"If you concocted me from your own imagination,

how is it that I know you are about to make a discovery that will change everything?"

"What are you talking about?"

"If I were to predict your future, would that prove to you that I am who I say I am?"

"You can't do that."

"Your current search is about to be over. Only for a new search—a more important one—to begin."

"Is it a rule—some kind of operating procedure? That you ghosts must speak in riddles, conundrums, and half-truths?"

Tilson Wayne—or whoever he was—laughed. Then he stood and simply walked away.

~ ~ ~

As I started back to find Jax, I heard someone crying in the forest.

"Who's out there?" I said loudly, silently praying it was Amanda.

"Help," was the reply. Distant. Somewhere in the inky blackness.

"Keep talking," I said. "Make some noise."

Nothing but silence. Whoever it was had too much fear that the murderous demons were still around, perhaps looking for them. This realization was as a spear pushed through my heart.

Amanda was incapable of such fear.

I kept walking toward the area I'd heard the voice, swinging my flashlight beam back and forth. Finally I heard another voice, different, even softer:

"I'm scared."

It was almost a whisper. I was close.

"My name is Detective Bobby Mac," I said. "I'm here with the good guys."

"Over here," the first voice said.

I moved the LED light toward the voice. There were three little girls, huddled together under two fallen trees. They were dirty, disheveled, and shivering. One of them was wearing a blood-stained, tattered dress—she had lost a shoe. The one that remained, though mangled and muddied, was clearly white.

~ ~ ~

We gathered the three girls together, fed them rations, and made them drink small amounts of water. They were clearly dehydrated and completely disoriented. All they seemed to remember was the mass attack that occurred at the staging area only hours before.

"What do we do?" Jax said.

His handful of deputies guarded the perimeter of the clearing, but it was a lackluster gesture. There were scores of FBI agents lying in pieces all around us. How much protection could half a dozen small town cops be? In fact, how much could anyone do?

I could not stop thinking about Amanda. She was dead. Before we really had a chance to grow together as one, she was out of my life forever. But I still needed to find her. What was left of her. It did not matter how long, or how much effort. I would stay there. After all, there was nothing left. Everything I cared about had been ripped from my life.

When we were kids, Paddy and Ma took us to mass

every Saturday. We attended Wednesday night bible study. The story of Job had always troubled me. The man was a devoted servant of God and yet the Lord rained down so much tragedy on the poor soul that he all but renounced his faith—he *did* renounce the day he was born. All for what? A kind of wager with Satan? A way for God to prove to the fallen angel the mettle of a follower?

My own mettle too seemed to have been tested all these years. Far beyond what any reasonable person would consider a breaking point. But in my case, what faith could God be testing? I wasn't sure I ever had any to begin with.

There certainly wasn't any left now.

"I'm sorry," Jax said, offering the girls some milk he'd warmed over the campfire.

I looked at him without answering. Hot tears ran down my cheeks. Tears of sorrow. Tears of mourning. Tears of anger and hate.

I had not cried since burying my wife on that wintry Denver morning. The realization made me even more resolute to never do it again. I wiped my eyes and walked away. I didn't want anyone to see me, least of all the children. What had I been through compared to them? They were *eleven-years*-old. Who knew the horror they'd witnessed this past week and a half?

There was no need to traumatize them any more than they already were. We needed to be their heroes. I needed to be that for them, as ludicrous as my heart knew that idea to be.

~ ~ ~

"What are you doing?" Tilson Wayne said to me, just beyond the circle of light from the fire.

"Leave me alone, ghost. I don't need your illusions anymore. I never did."

"Those girls are not illusions."

"Maybe not. But you are. You are an unwanted manifestation of my beleaguered mind."

"How could I have known that you would find them?"

"I can't answer that."

"You asked before why I had come."

"So?"

"I am no manifestation of your mind, Detective. I can't tell you exactly what I am, but I know that I am real. Yes, I died when I was eleven years old. What you see before you is a man I cannot explain any more than you can."

"So you are a confused ghost. Perfect."

"Like you, I am forced to question who I am. I don't like that. Yet I am aware of things—strangely aware of a purpose for me being here. I hate not having all the answers."

"We are too alike for you to be anything but my own inner demon."

"I have been brought here to tell you something. That the fight is winnable. Rule would never have you believe so, but it is."

"How could you think you know that? Because *God* sent you?"

"I am not sure I believe in God."

"We now have that in common, too."

"You've given up your faith?"

"I'm not sure what faith I ever had. I have always at

least believed there was a God. I am not sure I can any longer. What kind of father would allow *this* to happen to his children?" I said, gesturing to the killing field.

"What God would allow an eleven-year-old boy to be run over by a piece of his father's own farm equipment?" Wayne said.

"I once accepted that God took away my leg, and my wife. I'm not one to shirk my own responsibilities in things. We all have to bear an amount of suffering, and I was more than willing to bear mine. But I cannot reconcile what happened here tonight. This is more than anyone should have to bear. God cannot explain this one to me."

"I understand."

"Do you?"

"I do. But that doesn't change the fact that I am here to tell you that the fight is not *over*."

"You keep saying that."

"Because I know it to be true."

"How can you know *anything*? You don't even know who you are."

"I am a friend," he said. "Isn't that enough?"

"Disappear. You are nothing more than my subconscious wishing on a star."

"I will go," Wayne said. "But there is something you need to know before I do. Something I *do* remember."

"Tell me and then be gone."

"I want you to know my mother's maiden name."

~ ~ ~

Meyer West was locked away in the back corner of the

basement in the *William E. Borah Memorial Library*, nearly invisible behind the mountain of books. His eyes hurt. His back ached. His very soul begged him for a reprieve from the torrent of despicable history he'd been devouring for the past week. Terrible things. Unconscionable acts of torture. Rituals that would make the most stalwart sick.

But the answer was there. He knew it. And so he kept reading. Skipping meals. Drinking too little water. And now the toll was noticeable. He could no longer concentrate. And still, the only real clue he'd found was that of the three sisters. And that made no sense either. The missing girls were pre-adolescents, yes, but they were not sisters. According to the investigations, they were not even friends. Acquaintances did not fit the profile.

One last book, Meyer told himself. There was really only one last book he wanted to examine. Another on the language of the Coeur d'Alene tribe.

Where was it? He rooted through the books on the faux wood table, and through those that had either toppled to the floor or been resigned there.

It was there, somewhere, hiding from him, perhaps.

Then he found it.

And a sound jumped at him from the darkness.

"Hello?"

No answer.

Probably the night librarian, rummaging around and staying close so as to be at hand to remind him of closing time.

10 PM.

He knew. He did not need reminding. He'd closed the library down the past six nights. Tonight would be no different. But the gangly man who reminded Meyer of

Ichabod Crane would still come, scolding, chewing on Meyer as if he were a schoolboy hiding in the depths to avoid the teacher's gaze.

"I say, *hello.*"

Still nothing. And no more rummaging.

Meyer went back to his search and found the volume on languages. The Coeur d'Alene dialect was an extremely rare and complicated one. Translations were many times either completely contrived or varied. There was one term that seemed wrong to him now, after so much reading.

'm'mi'msh.

Little box.

Meyer found the reference in the story of an ancient sacrificial ritual retold—a slang reference to a pre-teen girl. But that reference now felt wrong. Out of context. The book he'd just relocated had more literal translations of many other words. Maybe...

BOOM.

A pile of books toppled to the floor in the darkness, not ten feet away.

"Who is it?" Meyer said. "I am well aware of the time, sir. Unless you are leaving early, I have at least another twenty minutes."

No response.

Meyer went back to the book, rifling through the pages, putting his photographic memory to the test. But he was *tired.* Not only physically and mentally but also *spiritually.* Too much evil; too much darkness.

And then he found it.

Exactly what he'd been looking for.

The needle in a pile of needles.

The original book he read that referenced the sacrifice of the children had a slightly different spelling of the

Coeur d'Alene word; a variation he'd not noticed before:

One extra letter; a second 'i'.

'm'mii'msh.

THAT was the word.

Meyer continued reading.

"Oh, dear," he muttered as the significance of the newer definition nestled slowly into his tattered mind. "This can't be…"

Before he could consider it further, the monster came for him out of the blackness—a creature from beyond his worst imagination.

~ ~ ~

The FBI and State Police took over the crime scene in the Coeur d'Alene forest. It was unavoidable. Melissa Grant and the other two girls were transported to the county Children's Services. Jax was not taking the federal and state intervention well, but even if he could have opposed it, neither one of us was in a condition to argue the logic.

We were each, in a word, devastated. Jax wanted to be with his family. With his girls. He wanted to release the township back to the comfort of their own homes. He needed his *town back*.

We both needed to be as far away as possible from the carnage north of Rocky Gap. Better that other agencies with stronger forensics teams work through the near insurmountable task there.

Back at the hotel, I used Meyer's spare key to enter his room. He'd not slept there. I remember thinking perhaps the librarian had allowed him to sleep off his exhaustion at the cubicle he'd commandeered since our arrival in Idaho. I decided to shower. I knew there was no sleep in my immediate future, so after cleaning up and downing a cup of coffee from the local barista shack, I drove over to the library.

I realized for the first time it was Sunday when I encountered the locked doors. I cannot explain the feeling that next came over me, but I was positive something had happened to my cousin. I moved around to the back of the library, to the loading dock. There was a door there with a standard knob, no deadlock. With a screwdriver from the truck I was able to jimmy the door.

I found Meyer in the lower level. When I first saw him I was convinced he was dead—that I had lost yet another loved one. My cousin was barely breathing. I called Jax and asked him to send an ambulance and to come by himself and meet me at the library.

Blood was spattered about the floor, spilled books, papers, and toppled shelves. I cannot say it looked like there had been much of a struggle. Clearly Meyer was no match for whatever had attacked him. The damage around him was caused by the assault, not by any valiant attempt by my cousin and friend to defend himself.

It was also clear that the intent was for him to die. The wounds to his body were mortal. Had I not come in to find him, he would have bled out by Monday morning when the librarian returned to open the building.

The paramedics arrived with Jax, and after they carted Meyer away, barely alive, my brother quizzed me:

"What the hell is going on? What *is* all this?"

"I'm not sure," I told him. "This has more to do with our family, I think."

"Like all we've seen is staged for our benefit."

"Exactly."

"Mice, running through a maze."

"What?" I said.

"Like we're mice. Being led exactly where they want us to go."

"I saw Tilson Wayne again."

"Where?"

"When we found the girls."

"What did he have to say?"

"There is no 'he'. I think I'm going crazy."

"This," he said, motioning to the destruction in the library. "*This* shit is crazy. Not you."

"You haven't heard what he suggested."

"Okay…"

"I think he implied that Amanda is still alive."

"And you think that is just wishful thinking on your part?"

"I know it is."

"You know what they say about paranoia."

"Just because I'm paranoid doesn't mean they aren't out to get me."

"Exactly."

"We need to get over to the hospital."

~ ~ ~

The surgeon saved my cousin's life. He'd lost a lot of blood, but somehow no internal organs had been permanently damaged. Jax and I waited in his room in the intensive care unit—waited for him to wake up and tell us what kind of monster had attacked him.

And, hopefully, why?

The doctor said he should wake up after the anesthesia wore off. He would be weak, and there was no guarantee his memory would not evade him, but it was likely we could at least speak with him.

It was several hours before Meyer woke up.

"I'm alive," he said through a dry, chafed throat.

"You've got a penchant for overstating the obvious," I told him.

"Welcome back," said Jax.

Meyer waved me closer. I put a few ice chips from a cup at his bedside into his mouth and he crunched them hungrily.

"There is a problem," he said. "I don't think Rule wants the girls."

"He doesn't," I said. "We found them."

Meyer shook his head.

"He doesn't want *those* girls," he managed.

"What are you saying?"

Meyer ate more ice.

"Yours," he said softly.

"What?"

"He wants *your* girls."

"Mine?" Jax said, and moved in close.

Meyer again shook his head. He was weak. Each word was a chore for him. He pointed at me.

"YOUR...girls...Mac."

"You're still woozy. I have no daughters. Jax...you are talking about my *brother*."

Jax did not attempt to hide his concern.

"Talk to us," he said.

I motioned for him to take it easy.

"What exactly did you learn?"

He pointed to a pen and pad on the portable table. I

handed both to him. Writing would be easier than trying to push out the words. He scribbled on the paper and then pushed the pad in my direction. The words he'd written caused my stomach to flip and my blood to stop flowing.

Not pre-teen.
<u>Unborn</u>.

14

JAX SECURED four mountain horses from a local outfitter, one for each of us plus two deputies. We decided the trip into the wilderness should be a small party. One, we would attract less attention. Large numbers would give us no advantage against the creatures we hunted. They cut through a hundred trained federal agents as if they were not even there.

The hope that Amanda was still alive had infused me with a new energy. I felt almost superhuman. Even if she was alive, the balance between her life and her death was no doubt delicate, but I had been given a chance to save her—I could not ask for more than that.

The translation Meyer found was more accurate than those he previously used. We'd been operating under the theory that Rule intended to sacrifice three pre-teen women; the reality was that he intended to kill three unborn MacAulays—three vessels that would one day produce more warriors in the sacred lineage. And their mother was to die with them. This was the prophecy foretold in the ancient Coeur d'Alene splinter rituals: that to destroy a lineage there must be a sacrifice to the fly god. And that sacrifice would happen that night—when the *one moon* rose to the middle of the sky, I would indeed lose the things most important to me.

"You mentioned that you felt you were going crazy," Jax said to me as we readied the horses.

"Why? Are you inclined to agree with me now?"

"Not necessarily."

"But…"

"It occurs to me that insanity might run in our family."

"That would be an ugly legacy," I said.

"The odds are terrible. We're facing an impossible situation."

"And yet we are still going forward."

"Yes."

"That is the crazy part, right?"

"No. Based on what you've seen—what I've seen, too—going forward isn't a choice. It's the only option available."

"You want to ask me about the crucifix."

"I can only assume you brought it with you for a reason."

"I did. Not sure I could tell you what that reason is now."

I knew the crucifix might be our only hope. I didn't like admitting that. It didn't make me feel any more rational now than it had back in Colorado, over a year ago, when my willingness to use it had saved all of us. I brought it because it might do the same for us now.

"How far to the pass?" I said.

"Nine miles," Jax said. "Maybe ten. It will take us all day."

"How far will we have to climb?"

"A few thousand feet. It'll get steep, but there's trail all the way to the top."

"The horses will be okay?"

"Better than we would be alone."

"How will we know which way to go?"

"I am hoping I can track them."

"You don't sound all that confident."

"Best option we have right now," he said.

"I have a feeling they won't be hiding from us."

"I figure the same thing."

~ ~ ~

Spence Grant waited for his opportunity. It was too long since he'd received any direction—any word at all—so he knew it was time to take action himself. His little girl had been found and relinquished into the hands of the county. He couldn't live with that. How could Annir have allowed such an aberration? That was not *the plan*.

Escape was relatively easy. The old deputy on the night shift—a road apple named Charlie Neil who was six months from the twilight of retirement—had become friendly with Spence. Well, Spence had lured him into a tactical friendship. The old man was lonely. When men get old, people stop listening to what they have to say. Spence simply filled a need. He talked to Charlie about the U of M Grizzlies. Fly fishing. Seasonal wildfires. Anything that mattered to the old fart.

And the time had come.

Spence lay down on the cold concrete floor and held his stomach.

"Charlie," Spence groaned through the bars of the jail cell.

The old deputy walked down the empty row.

"What's the problem, Spence?"

"What was in that food you brought me earlier?"

"Standard fare. Burger and fries from the diner, you know that."

"Think that meat might've been bad. Feeling more

133

than a little green."

"Let me get a doc," Charlie said.

"I think maybe some cold water first," Spence told him. "To splash on my face. I'm so hot."

"Sure, buddy. Let me see what I can do."

"Some of that Pepto, too, if you have any."

"Back in a minute," Charlie said and shuffled away.

Earlier Spence had placed two unopened cans of soda inside a pillowcase; bounty he'd squirreled away after occasions when the elderly jailer had forgot to open them prior to food service.

Charlie came back with a small bowl of water, a wet rag, and a bottle of pink stuff. He opened Spence's cell and walked in without a care. When he bent over to place the water bowl on the table, he turned his back on the prisoner. Spence stood quietly and swung the pillowcase in a long arc. The soda cans connected with Charlie at the base of his skull, killing him instantly. The deputy dropped to the floor in a lifeless heap.

Spence dragged the body deeper into the shadows of his cell, out of sight. He then disrobed the corpse and dressed himself in the uniform, which fit him well, if a bit short in the legs. The shoes were several sizes too small so Spence had no choice but to wear the laceless sneakers. He didn't plan on anyone seeing him up close, anyway—not until it was too late to squabble about his shoes.

He took the keys from Deputy Neil and stole a squad car. Charlie had let it slip a few nights earlier that Melissa was staying at a foster home on the east side of town. A family called Martinek. Spence Googled the address on the computer inside the police car. The drive took less than five minutes.

Spence knocked on the door at the Martinek house. If he could do things the easy way, he'd give it one shot. The porch light came on and a disheveled Tom Martinek answered.

"Officer," he said, still shaking the cobwebs from his head. "What's the trouble?"

"Melissa Grant's father has escaped," he told Martinek. "I need to check on the girl, make sure you all are okay."

"Sure, sure. Come in."

"Don't wake your wife," Spence said, keeping the flashlight in the man's eyes. "Just show me to the girl's room."

"This way," Martinek said.

Melissa was in deep sleep. Spence wanted to scoop her up into his arms.

"Officer?" Martinek said.

Spence turned around to see the man pointing at his jailhouse slip-on shoes.

"Ran out of the station without my boots," Spence said, and clocked Martinek across the forehead with the butt end of the big flashlight. He reached down and found a pulse. Blood ran from the wound in the man's head.

"Oh well," Spence whispered aloud. "Shouldn't have paid attention to the shoes."

Spence gathered some of Melissa's clothing from the dresser and closet—a pair of jeans, sweatshirt, tennis shoes, socks, and a stocking cap. Then he wrapped his daughter in the twin comforter and carried her out to the cop car. She never even woke up.

~ ~ ~

The first few hours of riding were uneventful. The trail wound monotonously through cold, shaded forest, sporadic fields where the sky opened and the sun warmed our bones again, and then back into the darkness. It seemed for every thousand feet of altitude we gained, the trail would wind down into another valley and we'd lose it. I tried to keep my senses keen, watching the peripheral, listening for anything to warn us of imminent attack.

It was coming. This I knew. When? How many? What we were to do? These were questions I couldn't answer. But we were not alone. We hadn't seen them yet, but I could sense their presence—hidden in the shadows, perhaps, but following us. Plotting. Anticipating. And all we could do was forge ahead.

Mice in a maze, Jax had called it.

My brother led the way. My horse was second and the two deputies, Severs and Unser, brought up the rear. The trail was narrow and soft from the rain earlier in the week. The air was damp and fecund. We saw no other wildlife at all and the only sound was the steady clomp of the horse's hoofs on the dead earth.

I couldn't stop thinking about Amanda. There had not been much time to consider the enormity of what was ahead. Rule's words haunted me:

This is not your God's world, or even your own. It is mine.

Meyer believed God was omniscient, all knowing. This implied a preordainment to what lay in wait for us somewhere in the wild distance. Could this be true? And if it was, why go forward? Why play out our predestined roles in this macabre drama?

It occurred to me then that we could just as easily be running through God's personal maze.

After we entered a large clearing, Jax raised a hand and pulled his horse to a halt. The sun seeped through the outer layer of clothing and when it reached my chilled flesh, the warmth made hope seem less distant. Jax dismounted and told us to do the same.

"They've got a hell of a jump on us," Jax said. "We'll be lucky to reach the peak before sunset."

"Then why are we stopping?" I said. He was making no sense.

Jax squatted, playing with loose sticks and pine needles on the ground. Without looking up, he motioned slightly toward the edge of the clearing, where the trail disappeared back into the dense forest. He spoke softly, without moving his lips.

"I saw movement up ahead."

I looked to the trees with my eyes, keeping my face down. It was too dark to see anything in the trees. Jax began drawing in the dirt with a stick. I stood and removed my canteen from the saddle. I took a short pull of cool water. I then slipped the Crucifix of Ardincaple from a pouch in the saddlebag on my horse.

"How many?" I said, squatting down next to my brother.

"Couldn't tell," Jax said.

"We don't have time to wait them out," I whispered.

"If they catch us in the trees, time won't matter."

I knew he was right, but the truth was they could have us in the trees any time they wanted.

"They could have attacked us any number of times."

"I think they want us here, in the open," Jax said.

"Which means they have numbers."

"Exactly."

"I don't understand," said Severs.

"The density of the forest evens the odds. In the open, they can split us up."

"Let's make a fire," Jax said. "Just cooking up some warm breakfast. Unser, I don't need oatmeal...I need three sticks of that dynamite you brought for me."

I looked at him with raised eyebrows.

"I didn't want to argue with you," Jax said. "You have your talisman, I have mine."

Severs and I gathered some twigs and small, broken limbs, and then cleared a small patch of dirt. I used the matches and a clump of the driest grass I could find to start the small fire. Jax poured water into a pot and laid the three sticks close on the ground. He removed three blasting caps and three fuses from a watertight case and began inserting them, one by one. Unser set the pot down in the coals at the edge of the fire and put on a show, stirring the water slowly.

I placed the crucifix next to the explosives. The other three stared at the ancient talisman.

"It was said to be forged from steel smelted from the nails used to crucify Christ," I said. "I can't explain what happened. And I don't have any idea how much of its history is truth and how much is legend. But I know what it did for us. It saved our lives."

"Can you call on its power again?" Jax said.

"I'm not sure. I think the power found *me*."

"Well, just in case..."

There was a CRASH at the far end of the clearing. The four of us rose to the sight of two-dozen dark, monstrous beasts bursting through the downfall at the edge of the far tree line. Their sizes and shapes differed, but they were each twisted with muscle and howling with hatred and rage.

Jax bent over and snatched one stick of dynamite. He quickly estimated the distance between the demons and where we stood. He needed to know where and when the dynamite would detonate. He clipped the fuse to an inch and a half. He put the end of the fuse in the fire and it ignited. We stood back as my brother heaved the projectile as far as he could. It landed ten yards in front of the mass of demons and detonated.

Earth, deadwood, and demon pieces blew skyward in an incredible fountain of destruction.

Severs had clipped another fuse and was already lighting a second stick as a dozen surviving creatures cleared the thick cloud of smoke and debris. They had fanned out in a wide line, no longer clustered stupidly.

The deputy threw the stick in a high arc—too high. It exploded a good ten feet in the air over the middle of the skirmish line of monsters. The concussion took out two of the beasts, putting them down hard, but ten more ran on. And they were too close to risk another detonation.

"Get behind me," I said, and held forth the Crucifix of Ardincaple. I showed it to the beasts as they gained ground, holding it before me like a shield, waiting for the power to surge forth and allow me to consume my enemies.

Nothing happened. The rusted dagger remained just that.

A useless artifact.

And the demons were nearly upon us.

"DRAW YOUR WEAPONS," Jax shouted, and the three of them fanned out to my right and left.

I pulled my Beretta and leveled the sights at the tall

monster that was leading the charge, putting the crosshair in the center of its bumpy, disfigured forehead. I squeezed off a round and the demon's head burst into a splash of blood and bone. The creature fell and skidded in the wet earth; its brethren trampled the dead thing without regard.

Jax and his deputies fired as well, cutting down three more. I fired again, hitting a short, fat demon in the center of its chest. A thick, hunched, corded beast reached Deputy Severs and tackled him. The two rolled along the ground, Severs in a kind of bear hug, and when the beast stood, it tore one of the deputy's outstretched arms from his body with a sickening crunch.

Severs screamed in agony. The demon threw him to the ground and dropped on top of his quaking body. The thing sank its long, gnashing teeth into his shoulder and neck—tearing, ripping, gorging.

I aimed carefully, not wanting to risk hitting Deputy Severs, but he wasn't going to survive much longer if his attacker was not stopped. I pulled the trigger and caught the demon in the back of his skull, the force of the 9MM flipping the beast, head over tail.

Before I could try to reach our fallen man, a demon lunged for Jax. My brother ducked at the last moment and the beast missed him, tumbling to the ground behind. Jax spun, leveled himself, and we both fired.

Unser had killed one more; the four remaining demons ran for the nearest forest edge. Jax scooped up the last stick of dynamite, clipped half the fuse, lit it, and threw it past the scrambling beasts. It landed between them and the tree line and blew them to hell.

Deputy Severs could not be saved. He was dead when we returned to him, his body having given in to shock.

140

Jax was visibly affected. Losing a brother or sister cop is never easy. That said, his sudden anger toward me was still surprising.

"What the fuck good is that thing?" he said, pointing to the crucifix.

"I don't know. I really don't..."

"You say it saved you! It did nothing for my deputy. NOTHING."

"I know that, Jax..."

"I knew Bill Severs for twenty-five years. He was my friend."

"I'm sorry."

"You're sorry and he's dead. Kind of a shitty trade."

"Fuck you, Jax. I didn't kill him."

Jax looked up at me, eyes red, swollen, and accusatory.

"But you thought you could stop it, didn't you?"

"I wasn't sure."

"Well you damn sure had US believing."

"I did what I could."

My words sounded as hollow as I felt.

"Put that thing away," he said. "It's a joke."

"We need to get moving."

"Not until we bury him."

"Call for someone," I said.

"We're not going anywhere until we give my friend a decent burial."

"I'm not trying to be callused. We don't have the tools. Or the time."

"You and Unser go on then," my brother said, grabbed the water pot, and started to dig.

"I'm not going anywhere," said Unser. He grabbed a thick, pointed stick and began scraping at the wet earth.

I put the Crucifix of Ardincaple back into the

saddlebag and found my own makeshift shovel. We worked at burying Deputy Severs as the sun continued to move mercilessly across the cloudless sky.

~ ~ ~

"I'm sorry," Jax said when we were back riding the trail.

"If I could have left without you, I would have. I'm sorry about Severs, but this is Amanda's life we're talking about."

"I couldn't just walk away. But you're right. I let my emotions take over. It won't happen again."

"I get it. But we've lost time—how much further to the fork?"

The highline trail we followed would eventually split into three separate paths, one for each of the Three Sisters Peaks.

"Four or five hours," Jax said, looking at his watch and for any weather in the skies. "What are the chances we'll run into more of, uh, them?"

"I doubt we will. Of course, that's just my gut."

"Care to expand on that?"

"I think that was just a message."

"What message?"

"Hello. Welcome to the game."

"Nice. This Rule asshole is a real specimen."

"I can't say I'm happy you're going to meet him."

"Me either."

We rode in silence for a bit. I knew, however, that my brother's mind was in high gear. And I knew the questions that were stalking around in his head like

142

combat boots on broken glass.

"I can't explain what happened back there," I said. "Or what didn't happen."

"I know you can't."

"It went down in Colorado just as I told it."

"I believe you."

"Severs should be alive right now. I failed him."

"You didn't fail him. And you didn't kill him."

"How am I supposed to save Amanda now?"

"What?"

"The crucifix was our only real hope. We can't save Amanda without it."

"We'll just have to rely on ourselves."

"Ourselves?"

"Good over evil. We're going to have to believe in that."

"And if we can't believe?"

"Then Rule has already won."

We did not encounter any more resistance. We rode through the heat of middle day and on into late afternoon. We reached the trail's fork with maybe two hours of daylight remaining. Jax climbed down from his mount and knelt in the trail, examining the ground carefully. He didn't need to. Rule and his legions made no effort to disguise their route.

"Pretty obvious they went this way," he said, pointing down the rightmost trail.

"Deer Song," Unser said.

"What's that?" I said.

"Each of the peaks themselves has a name," Jax told me. "This one was named after a Coeur d'Alene squaw that was murdered in her teepee by the United States Cavalry."

"Great history, ours," I said.

"Not *my* history. Yours either."

The three of us rode toward Deer Song peak, what little confidence remained fading a little more with each mile we covered. Just before the trail climbed out of the trees into the low-vegetation of our remaining ascent, Jax stopped us.

"There's no more cover," he said quietly. "From here forward we won't be surprising anyone. Or any*thing*."

"They know we're here," I said.

Jax looked at his deputy.

"This is beyond duty now, Donnie. I can't order you to go this last mile."

"You don't need to," Unser said.

"I had to say it," Jax told him.

Unser nodded, but the fear in his eyes betrayed what we were all feeling.

As we rode slowly from the cover of the trees, the land around us took on the look of the lunar landscape. The horse's hoofs crunched as they picked their way amongst the loose shale. Above us, lining the winding, open trail, were the demons—creatures of every size, shape, and dark color. They sat on the rocks, hung from the cliff faces—they were *everywhere*. Thousands, perhaps. All watching us. Hungering for us. But none attacked. They simply stared—eyeing their prey, willing us to keep moving forward, deeper into their domain.

As we climbed, the trail took us closer to them—close enough to see the bottomless hatred in their eyes; close enough to hear them wheezing and growling and scraping their claws across the boulders and stones beneath them.

We tried to avoid looking at them directly. To stare too long would erode what little courage remained. Clearly this was part of the setup. The next move in Father Rule's chess match. He did not have to let us through. We'd never stand up to another dozen of these creatures, much less thousands. Rule could have us now, and that realization brought a strange calm over me.

If I was to die, then it should be here, with Amanda, with our babies—there was no longer any doubt in my mind that she was out there, somewhere ahead of us. I wouldn't have gone back even if that were an option. I knew Jax and Donnie felt the same way. We'd already lost too much. And leaving wouldn't solve a thing. Somehow we needed to end this.

The final climb was extremely steep, even for horses bred to move through such inhospitable terrain. At times it felt as if we were going straight up. And there was never a moment when we were not surrounded by Rule's army. I never looked backward, but I sensed the demons we'd already passed joining together, following us up the mountain.

~ ~ ~

Deer Song Peak was incredibly flat, about as large as a basketball court. As the horses reached the top they halted, refusing to go any further. At the far end of the peak was a group that no doubt had our animals spooked.

Rule was standing there. And the demon Annir. Three other misshapen monsters guarded them on either side.

And there was Amanda.

She was alive, seated on a cracked boulder. Trembling, she looked to be in deep shock, perhaps only kept conscious by her captors. The desire to rush to her side overwhelmed me, held in check only by my hatred of Father Rule. I had to keep my head. If we were to have any chance, cool heads were a necessity.

The group of them could not have been more than a step or two from the north edge of the mountain peak. How far was the drop?

Two thousand feet?

Three?

We stayed our ground at the other end of the peak, just at the mouth of the trail, trying desperately to put the guttural sounds behind us from our mind. We were not safe. We were exactly where Rule and his army of darkness wanted us to be.

And I had no idea what our next move should be. Never mind that the Crucifix of Ardincaple had proved worthless. And we could never reach Rule, not before he killed Amanda and the babies she carried.

"Macaulay," Rule called, his voice barely above the rising wind.

"We've come," I said. "Just like you wanted."

"You and your brother, come closer. Over here."

"I don't suppose you'd consider taking me in exchange for my...for Agent Byrne?"

"I think you know the game better than that."

I looked to Jax and he nodded.

"Wait here," he said to Donnie.

We walked toward Rule. As we did, demons from below on the trail began climbing to the peak, swallowing the deputy from view and filling the space between him and us. For every few feet we advanced, our escape was closed off from the rear.

"I wanted you close," Rule said when we stopped a few yards away. "We finish this soon."

"This is no game, Rule."

"You're wrong. This has always been a game. Since before your memories. Since before all of you. For all of time, the game has been played."

"None of this matters," I said.

"It matters to *you*," he hissed.

I reached behind me and slipped the crucifix from my belt, where I had hidden it at our last stop. I held it before him, my hand wrapped around the hilt.

"Remember this?" I said to the beast.

"You've discovered its power?"

"I have."

"You are a poor liar, cop. The weakness of your faith bleeds out in your words. Your ancestors forged a weapon whose power is only as strong as the belief of he who wields it."

"If you kill her," I said. "I'll take you down, too."

Rule smiled wickedly. His blackened, razor-like teeth absorbing the fading sunlight.

"I wish you were that much of a challenge to me. I do. I relish such tests. But your trepidation betrays you. Your faith was never strong enough. You are too reasonable."

"Reasonable?"

"You could never put your confidence in a God who would allow the death of innocents."

"My confidence—my faith—is in the idea that evil such as yourself will be stopped. In the end I'm just a cop, Rule. We're stubborn that way. We each have such faith."

"The field has never been that balanced," Rule said. "You think in terms of fairness and of honor. Such ideals must exist for good to have any chance against evil. I told you before, this is *my world*. God is not here. He never was."

Rule pointed and the demons took us. The rest of the horde—dozens of Rule's disciples—retreated to the far end of the mountaintop.

The sun was quickly dropping in the west and the chill night air was already seeping in.

"The moon rises in less than an hour," Rule said.

"The one moon."

"It's a silly superstition. But it is one I will honor for this, our special occasion. The next phase in the game."

"Why do any of this?" I said. "You said it yourself. This is your world. Why not simply take what you want?"

"Taking has no discernible effect on the spirit," Rule said. "I desire to *break you*. You and all like you."

"You'll only strengthen my resolve," I said.

"What little faith you may have had once has died. Resolve is doomed without faith. And I will have you witness the destruction of your own seed. I will extinguish that light in you forever. Everything you are will be lost."

"And what about me?" Jax said. It was the first time he'd made a sound since we arrived.

"You have a much different fate ahead of you, Jackson."

"Don't call me that."

"You ask about yourself, but you already know the answer, don't you?"

"I have no idea what you mean," said Jax.

"You are weaker than your brother," Rule told him.

"Since childhood, you've known this. Spent your whole life denying it. But denial cannot wipe away the truth, no matter how much you wish it were so."

"Fuck you, demon."

"You're second chair to your brother. You always have been. Surely you'd like an opportunity to change that."

Jax said nothing.

"All roads lead to this one," Rule said.

He motioned to Annir, who leaped up and snatched Jax from the grip of the lesser demon. My brother struggled mightily, but was as helpless as a child in the arms of a grizzly bear. The huge demon put Jax down hard, pressing him against the ancient, stony ground.

"More power than you've ever imagined, Jackson," Rule said, leering at me as he walked toward my brother. "You'll never be found wanting in the company of your big brother. Not ever again."

Rule straddled my brother, further pinning him on the hard ground. He ripped Jax's shirt—tore it away from his body and tossed it behind him, where Annir took it and tied my arms behind me. The demon then pulled me over next to my brother, forcing me to my knees, only inches away from Jax's twisted face.

Rule then raised his right hand in the air. His skeletal, spindly fingers ended in long, straight, knife-like claws. Jax screamed as the monster bent over him, pressing the talon on his index finger against the center of my brother's chest. He held it there for a moment and a single drop of blood emerged from Jax's skin and ran down his side to the cold earth below. Rule then leaned even further down, his face nearly touching Jax's, and slowly pushed the nail deep into the center of my

149

brother's chest right into the meaty core of his wild, beating heart.

The screaming began to die away, ending in a final, defeated whimper. And then there was nothing but the whistling wind. Jax lay there, silent, tears running down his cheek from eyes that were closed forever. Then Rule did something strange. He pressed his cracked, scabby lips against my dead brother's mouth and kissed him. He breathed into my brother's mouth, as if trying to revive him in a kind of macabre resuscitation. Rule's black eyes rolled into his head and he blew harder—pushing the life of the damned into my brother.

Then he ceased, and moved away from the limp body.

At first, nothing happened. And then Jax drew breath in his once dead lungs and coughed. Then he coughed again, harder.

His eyes opened. He slowly sat up.

He looked fine. As if nothing had happened. Then his eyes met mine, and I saw that they lacked any light at all.

"Big brother," he said, the words oozing from his lips. "Jackson…"

"You see now, don't you, my son?" Rule said.

Jax peered up at the demon with a strange gratitude in his countenance.

"I do. I see."

"What have you *done*, Rule?" I called out to him, horrified.

"Nothing that could have been done without his deep hatred of you. I only breathed a life into him that was already there, dormant, dreaming of freedom."

"This isn't you," I pleaded to my brother. "Think of your girls. Gracie. Celia. Your wife."

"This IS me," Jax said, climbing to his feet. "You've

150

never had the vision to see it. I've never had the courage to *release it.*"

"I want you to do something for me, son," Rule said to Jax.

Jax turned to him again, subservient.

"Anything."

Rule waved his hand and a far demon brought Deputy Unser out of the night, locked in its grip.

Jax looked into Father Rule's eyes and nodded. The demon handed the deputy over to my brother.

"Jax!" Unser screamed.

Jax grabbed Unser by the throat and by his belt, hoisting him high in the air.

"Jesus, Jackson," I shouted, trying to connect with what was left of my brother inside this new demon. "DON'T."

Jax never hesitated, not even for a moment. Donnie Unser sensed the end and fought desperately for his life, kicking and swinging his fists, raining blow after blow down on an oblivious captor. Donnie was no match for Jax, who now had the demonic strength of the damned.

The thing that used to be my brother walked slowly over to the edge of forever, as if savoring this moment— wanton to carry out its new master's command.

"NO JAX," I yelled one final time.

Paying me no heed, Jax reared back and threw his screaming, begging deputy out into the open maw of the abyss.

Then he turned around and smiled at me—the same kind of warped, psychotic smile I'd seen a hundred times on the faces of murderers and thugs and rapists. The same smile I'd seen on Eb Durning before they executed him in front of me.

The smile of Spence Grant.

The thing before me no longer resembled the brother I'd known.

"The moon has risen," Rule said. "Join us, cop, won't you?"

Annir growled and put his hands on my shoulders to bring me closer. The demon was strong but had no idea that I'd loosened the torn shirt used to tie my wrists. As the beast bent over to lift me, I drove the back of my skull into its mangled face.

Annir tossed his head back in rage and pain, but he was quick—one massive clawed hand swiped at me as I tried to roll away. Several claws tore through me, removing a piece of my left shoulder. I cried out in pain but kept rolling, putting distance between Annir and myself.

Then I saw it. Lying on the ground, just a few yards away.

The Crucifix of Ardincaple.

I lunged for it. Just as my hand wrapped around the hilt, a throng of crazed demons charged me, ready to take me apart. Father Rule was yelling to them, working them into a frenzied hunger. I came to my feet, blood flowing from the wound on my shoulder, the crucifix in my hand, and as I brought the weapon to bear the demons stopped suddenly, terrified of the talisman I held before me.

I kept it there, holding them back. Rule yelled to Annir to kill me now and the beast started moving slowly toward me. I could now see reluctance in those hateful eyes and maybe, what? Fear?

Annir was not as certain as his master was; worried perhaps that the weapon of my ancestors still held some power.

"KILL HIM," Rule commanded.

Obeying his master, Annir moved quickly toward me, fangs and claws bared. I pulled back the dagger, preparing to strike down the evil thing.

I put all my fears out of my mind, allowing my mind to free itself and to connect with the power I had summoned before. I willed the hero inside to spring forth and bring the weapon of MacAulay to life.

Nothing happened.

Annir was nearly upon me and the crucifix was cold and dead in my hand!

There was a sudden movement from behind me and the Crucifix of Ardincaple was at once gone from my hand. What happened next was a blur. Light exploded all around us, casting faux daylight across the mountaintop. The throng of hideous monsters all dropped to their knees in fear, disfigured, hairy arms shielding their eyes from the blinding light of God.

Someone was using the crucifix, fighting Annir toe-to-toe, the weapon having once again transformed into a mighty broadsword.

Tilson Wayne swung the sword, cutting piece after piece from the howling Annir. Rule beckoned and the prostrate demons began rising again, more afraid of their master than the great talisman in Wayne's hands. They rushed him by the dozen. Annir was already dead at the warrior's feet. Wayne turned to face the attackers coming fast to kill him.

One after one, the demons reached Tilson Wayne, and one by one he cut them down. The beasts exploded into brilliant clouds of fire and ash as the Crucifix of Ardincaple took their lives.

I turned to make sure Amanda was all right and saw three hunched, misshapen demons running toward her, ready to pounce.

"Tilly," I cried, and raised an open hand in the air.

Wayne had fought off the final onslaught and reacted instantly. He threw the sword toward me. Time slowed in my mind. I saw the beautiful weapon of my ancestors clearly as it flew through the air, end over end, and I caught it firmly in my grasp.

The power of Ardincaple instantly burst forth into my veins. I felt a thousand feet tall. I spun and decapitated the first demon, then dropped low, avoiding the outstretched claws of the second, cutting its legs from under it. The third demon froze after seeing its brethren explode into nothingness and I lunged forward, burying the blade deep into its black core. The last demon cried out and burst into flame.

The scores of demons at the fringes of Deer Song Peak faded back like cowards into the night. Only Father Rule remained.

I walked over to Tilson Wayne and stared him in the face.

He pointed a finger at Rule.

"Over half a century ago, demon, you stole my birthright from me."

"Who are you?" Rule said, confused and afraid for the first time.

"You don't remember me? Perhaps my father: Percival Wayne."

Recognition flickered in the beast's black eyes.

"Impossible."

"And my mother. Say her name, demon."

"You cannot be here," Rule said.

"Say it," Tilson Wayne said to Rule. "I want you to say her name so that they all hear it before you die."

Rule said nothing.

"Bobby?" Wayne said, eyes still on Rule. "Say her name."

I looked across space at my brother, who was opposite Father Rule now.

"Agnes *Macaulay*."

Wayne put his hand out flat, palm up, fingers spread. I placed the Crucifix of Ardincaple back in his grip. He walked toward Father Rule.

"*This*, is my destiny," he told the demon priest. "YOU are my destiny."

Wayne stepped between Jax and Rule.

"No," Rule said. "You're wrong."

The monster rushed him, and just as Wayne was about to cut him down, Rule ducked, sliding along the hard ground, then sprang back up to his feet and kept running, straight toward my brother.

Realization hit me like a locomotive.

"NO," I screamed as Rule threw open his arms and caught Jax, lifting him into the air and running them both off the edge of the cliff, down into three thousand feet of terminal night.

I ran to the edge, out of my mind.

My brother was gone.

There was nowhere for the two of them to have landed—nowhere but for several thousand feet below.

There was no more sound. I couldn't speak. The demon hordes had retreated back to the bowels of Hell from where they came. It was as if time had frozen—I wasn't sure I ever wanted it to begin again. Then I remembered Amanda. I spun around and she was on her feet, tears streaming down her ashen face.

But she was alive.

And my girls were safe.

Relief washed over me. I felt something—the presence of God? Whatever it was, for the first time in over a year I could see my future on the horizon, and I could see hope.

But then came a crushing sorrow on my heart. The recognition of the sacrifice I'd made; the enormous cost of my future.

A future in which I would never see my brother again.

Epilogue

MEYER RECOVERED fully. Amanda was transported to Kootenai Medical Center in Coeur d'Alene. The doctors there ran a slew of tests on her and the babies. All seemed well. After a few days, she, too, was released, and the three of us drove back to Denver.

I did see Tilson Wayne one more time. I had taken Tina and Sketch to the dog park near our home. I was sitting on a bench, throwing a ball while the two of them made a game out of stealing it from each other.

"Things are good again," Wayne said, suddenly appearing next to me. He looked younger, a version of him in his twenties, perhaps. Another part of his life he'd never know.

"I was wondering if I would see you again," I told him.

"I'm sorry for your loss."

"It's funny," I said. "In life, I had not reached out to Jax in *years*. How can a person who was no longer a part of my life leave such an enormous void?"

"You were kidding yourself to think he wasn't part of you any longer."

"I suppose so."

"How are they coping—his family, I mean?"

"It's a nightmare for them. I think Trish is going to

move the girls to Maine. Back with her family. There is too much sorrow and too many unanswerable questions in Idaho."

"For you, too."

"I've learned not to ask questions when I know there aren't any answers that will do."

"I told you once that the game is never over."

"You didn't have to tell me."

"You knew it already."

"You forget that I am a detective."

"I came back because I wanted to thank you," Wayne said.

"Thank me?"

"My purpose has finally been fulfilled. I can be at peace now. You were a big part of that."

"Only because I failed. It was the failure of my own faith that caused all of this. My brother died because of it."

"No. You said it yourself: you are a detective. You know there's a bigger picture here."

"I *do* realize that, Tilson. But honestly, it doesn't help me feel less culpable."

"I understand. But I thank you anyway."

"You are welcome, ghost."

"Love those daughters of yours, Bobby Mac."

Then the sun glared in my eyes and he was gone.

Before I had time to consider what he'd said, my cell phone rang in my pocket.

"Macaulay," I answered.

"Detective."

"Who is this?"

"How soon you forget. I thought we were friends."

"Grant?"

"Call me Spence."

"How did you get this number?"

"You're in the police computer."

"What the hell does that mean?"

"They didn't tell you."

"Tell me what?"

"I'm sorry about your brother. He was a good man."

"Where are you, Spence?"

"I needed to get away from Idaho for a while. Thought I would check out Denver. Such a nice town. And big."

"Your daughter…"

"With me," Spence said. "There's still a bigger plan afoot."

"How did you get out?"

"Come on, Mac. It was like Mayberry RFD up there."

"Meet me somewhere, Spence. Just me. We can talk this out."

"I'll be in touch, Mac. Say hello to your lovely girlfriend for me."

And he disconnected.

I sat there in stunned silence.

Spence Grant had escaped. He had Melissa.

Sketch brought me the ball. He stared at me expectantly, no greater care in the world, just a red ball and a majestic Colorado morning. His sister waited a few steps behind, tongue hanging, tail wagging.

Closing my eyes, I banished all the evil thoughts from my mind. I was just Bobby Mac. A man and his dogs. I opened my eyes and threw the ball as hard as I could across the dewy, glistening grass. Two rooster tails of water sprayed the air as the dogs ran to catch up.

ABOUT THE AUTHOR

R. S. Guthrie has been writing long fiction for several years. **Black Beast** is the first in the current series of *Clan of MacAulay* books featuring Denver Detective Bobby Macaulay.

L O S T is the second book in the Mystery-Detective series. Guthrie is writing a third book that will close out the popular *Clan of MacAulay* trilogy (though it will *not* be the final Detective Bobby Mac book).

Guthrie finished his magnum opus—a contemporary western mystery/thriller novel entitled *Dark Prairies*, set in a fictional town in his home state of Wyoming—in 2012. An prerelease excerpt was featured in the June 2011 issue of *New West*. The full book was published in July of 2012.

The author currently lives in Colorado with his beautiful wife, Amy, three Australian Shepherds, and a Chihuahua who *thinks* she is a forty-pound Aussie. It is a widely known fact that the canines rule the Guthrie household.

You can visit R.S. Guthrie at his author website (**http://www.rsguthrie.com**), his blog *Rob on Writing* (**http://robonwriting.com**), or at his author charity showcase: *Read a Book, Make a Difference* website (**http://RABMAD.com**).

artwork by Brent Dawson

artwork by Brent Dawson